D0788281

OUT OF THE WOODS

Stories

Chris Offutt

Simon & Schuster

SIMON & SCHUSTER
Rockefeller Center
1230 Avenue of the Americas
New York, NY 10020

This book is a work of fiction. Names, characters, places, and incidents either are products of the author's imagination or are used fictitiously. Any resemblance to actual events or locales or persons, living or dead, is entirely coincidental.

Copyright © 1999 by Chris Offutt
All rights reserved, including the right of reproduction in whole or in part in any form.

SIMON & SCHUSTER and colophon are registered trademarks of Simon & Schuster Inc.

Designed by Sam Potts
Manufactured in the United States of America
1 3 5 7 9 10 8 6 4 2

Library of Congress Cataloging-in-Publication Data
Offutt, Chris, [date]
Out of the woods : stories / Chris Offutt.
p.   cm.
Contents: Out of the woods — Melungeons — Moscow, Idaho — Two-eleven all around — High water everywhere — Barred owl — Target practice — Tough people.
1. United States—Social life and customs—20th century—Fiction.
2. Kentucky—Social life and customs—Fiction. I. Title.
PS3565.F387O98   1999
813'.54—dc21   98-43041
                                                        CIP
ISBN 0-684-82556-2

These stories have appeared in varying forms in the following magazines: "Out of the Woods" in *Esquire*; "Melungeons" and "Tough People" in *Story*; "Moscow, Idaho" in *Granta*; "Two-Eleven All Around" in *Glimmer Train*; "High Water Everywhere" in *GQ*; "Barred Owl" in *DoubleTake*; "Target Practice" in *Oxford American*. "Melungeons" also appeared in *Best American Short Stories 1994*.

For Rita,
Sam,
and
James

Contents

Where you come from is gone, where you thought you were going to never was there, and where you are is no good unless you can get away from it.

—*Flannery O'Connor,*
Wise Blood

OUT OF THE
WOODS

Out of the Woods

Gerald opened his front door at dawn, wearing only a quickly drawn-on pair of jeans. His wife's four brothers stood in the ground fog that filtered along the ridge. The oldest brother had become family spokesman after the father's death, and Gerald waited for him to speak. The mother was still boss but everything had to filter through a man.

"It's Ory," the oldest one said. "He got shot and is in the hospital. Somebody's got to fetch him."

The brothers looked at Gerald from below their eyebrows. Going after Ory wasn't a chore anyone wanted, and Gerald was new to the family, married to Kay, the only sister. He still needed to prove his worth. If he brought Ory home, maybe they'd cut the barrier that kept him on the edge of things, like he was nothing but a third or fourth cousin.

"Where's he at?" Gerald said.

"Wahoo, Nebraska. Ory said it would take two days but was easy to find."

"My rig won't make it."

"You can take the old Ford. She'll run till doomsday."

"Who shot him?"

The oldest brother flashed him a mean look. The rest were back to looking down, as if they were carpenters gauging the amount of linoleum needed for a job.

"Some woman," the oldest brother said.

Kay began to cry. The brothers left and Gerald sat on the couch beside Kay. She hugged her knees and bit a thumbnail, gasping in a throaty way that reminded him of the sounds she made in bed. He reached for her. She shrugged from his hand, then allowed his touch.

"Him leaving never made sense," Kay said. "He hadn't done nothing and nobody was after him. He didn't tell a soul why. Just up and went. Be ten years come fall."

"I'll go get him," Gerald whispered.

"You don't care to?"

"No."

"For my brothers?"

"For you."

She snuggled against him, her damp face pressed to his neck. She was tiny inside the robe. He opened the front and she pushed against his leg.

The next day he left in the black pickup. Gerald was thirty years old and had never been out of the county. He wore a suit that was snug in the shoulders, and short in the legs. It had belonged to his father, but he didn't figure anyone would notice. He wished he owned a tie. The dogwoods and redbuds had already lost their spring color. The air was hot. Four hours later he was in Indiana, where the land was flat as a playing card. There was nowhere to hide, no safety at all. Even the sun was too bright. He didn't understand how Ory could stand such open ground.

Illinois was equally flat but with less green to it. Gerald realized that he was driving through a sea-

son, watching spring in reverse. The Illinois dirt
was black as manure and he pulled over to examine
it. The earth was moist and rich. It smelled of life.
He let it trickle between his fingers, thinking of the
hard clay dirt at home. He decided to stop and get
some of this good dirt on the way back.

He drove all day and crossed the Mississippi
River at night. At a rest area, he unrolled a blanket
and lay down. He was cold. Above him the stars
were strewn across the sky. They seemed to be
moving down, threatening to press him against the
ground. Something bright cut across the night, and
he thought someone had shot at him until he realized it was a shooting star. The hills at home
blocked so much sky that he'd never seen one. He
watched the vast prairie night until fading into
sleep.

The eerie light of a flatland dawn woke him
early. The sun wasn't visible and the world seemed
to glow from within. There were no birds to hear.
He could see his breath. He drove west and left the
interstate at Wahoo and found the hospital easily. A
nurse took him to a small room. Everything was
white and the walls seemed to emit a low hum. He

couldn't place the smell. A man came into the room wearing a white coat. He spoke with an accent.

"I am Dr. Gupte. You are with the family of Mr. Gowan?"

"You're the doctor?"

"Yes." He sighed and opened a manila folder. "I'm afraid Mr. Gowan has left us."

"Done out, huh. Where to?"

"I'm afraid that is not the circumstance."

"It's not."

"No, he had a pulmonary thromboembolism."

"Is that American?"

"I'm afraid you will excuse me."

Dr. Gupte left the room and Gerald wondered who the funny little man really was. He pulled open a drawer. Inside was a small mallet with a triangular head made of rubber, perfect for nothing. A cop came in the room, and Gerald slowly closed the drawer.

"I'm Sheriff Johnson. You the next of kin?"

"Gerald Bolin."

They watched each other in the tiny room under the artificial light. Gerald didn't like cops. They got to carry a gun, drive fast, and fight. Anybody else got thrown in the pokey for doing the same thing.

"Dr. Gupte asked me to come in," the sheriff said.

"He really is a doctor?"

"He's from Pakistan."

"Run out of your own, huh."

"Look, Mr. Bolin. Your brother-in-law got a blood clot that went to his lung. He died from it."

Gerald cleared his throat, scanned the floor for somewhere to spit, then swallowed it. He rubbed his eyes.

"Say he's dead."

The sheriff nodded.

"That damn doctor ain't worth his hide, is he."

"There's some things to clear up."

The sheriff drove Gerald to his office, a small space with a desk and two chairs. A calendar hung from the wall. The room reminded Gerald of the hospital without the smell.

"Ory was on a tear," the sheriff said. "He was drinking and wrecked his car at his girlfriend's house. She wouldn't let him in and he broke the door open. They started arguing and she shot him."

"Then he got a blood clot."

The sheriff nodded.

"Did he not have a job?" Gerald said.

"No. And there's some money problems. He went through a fence and hit a light post. He owed back rent at a rooming house. Plus the hospital."

"Car bad hurt?"

"It runs."

"Did he own anything?"

"Clothes, a knife, suitcase, a little twenty-two pistol, a pair of boots, and a radio."

"What all does he owe?"

"Twelve hundred dollars."

Gerald walked to the window. He thought of his wife and all her family waiting for him. They'd given him a little money, but he'd need it for gas on the ride back.

"Can I see her?" he said.

"Who?"

"The woman that shot him."

The sheriff drove him a few blocks to a tan building made of stone. Near the eaves were narrow slits to let light in. They went through heavy doors into a common room with a TV set and a pay phone. Four cells formed one wall. A woman sat on a bunk in one of the cells, reading a magazine. She wore an orange jumpsuit that was too big for her.

"Melanie," the sheriff said. "You have a visitor. Ory's brother-in-law."

The sheriff left and Gerald stared through the bars. Her hair was dark purple. One side was long, the other shaved. Each ear had several small gold hoops in a row that reminded Gerald of a guide for a harness. A gold ring pierced her left nostril. She had a black eye. He wanted to watch her for a long time, but looked at his boots instead.

"Hidy," he said.

She rolled the magazine into a tube and held it to her good eye, looking at Gerald.

"I come for Ory," Gerald said, "but he's died on me. Just thought I'd talk to you a minute."

"I didn't kill him."

"I know it."

"I only shot him."

"A blood clot killed him."

"Do you want to screw me?"

Gerald shook his head, his face turning red. She

seemed too young to talk that way, too young for jail, too young for Ory.

"Let me have a cigarette," she said.

He passed one through the bars and she took it without touching his hand. A chain was tattooed around her wrist. She inhaled twin lines of smoke from her mouth into her nose. The ash was long and red. She sucked at the filter, lifting her lips to prevent them from getting burned. She blew a smoke ring. Gerald had never seen anyone get so much out of a single cigarette.

"Wish it was menthol," she said. "Ory smoked menthol."

"Well."

"What do you want," she said.

"I don't know. Nothing I don't guess."

"Me neither, except out of here."

"Don't reckon I can help you there."

"You talk just like Ory did."

"How come you to shoot him?"

"We had a fight, and he like, came over drunk. He wanted something he gave me and I wouldn't give it back. It was mine. He busted the lock and started tearing everything up, you know, looking for it. I had a little pistol in my vanity and I like, got it out."

Melanie finished the cigarette and he gave her another one, careful not to look at the ring in her nose. Behind her was a stainless steel toilet with a sink on top where the tank should be. When you washed your hands, it flushed the toilet. He thought of the jail at home with its putrid hole in the floor and no sink at all.

"What was it he was wanting so bad?"

"A wig," she said. "It was blond and he liked me to wear it. Sometimes I wore it in bed."

"You shot him over a wig."

"I was scared. He kept screaming, 'Give me back my wig.' So I, you know, shot him. Just once. If I knew he'd get that blood clot, I wouldn't have done it."

Gerald wondered how old she was but didn't want to insult her by asking. He felt sorry for her.

"He give you that eye?"

"The cops did. They think me and Ory sell dope but we don't, not really. Nothing heavy. Just to, like, friends."

"Why do you do that?" he said.

"Deal?"

"No. Cut your hair and stick that thing in your nose."

"Shut up," she said. She began yelling. "I don't need you. Get away from me. Get out of here!"

The sheriff came into the common room and took Gerald outside. The sky was dark with the smell of rain. He wanted to stand there until the storm swept over him, rinsing him of the jail. He underwent a sudden sense of vertigo, and for a moment he didn't know where he was, only that he was two days from anything familiar. He didn't even know where his truck was.

"She's a hard one," the sheriff said.

"I don't want no charges pressed against her."

"That's not up to you."

"She didn't kill him."

"I don't know about Kentucky," the sheriff said, "but in Nebraska, shooting people's a crime. Look, there's been a big wreck on Ninety-two and five people are coming to the hospital. They need the space. We got to get your brother-in-law to a funeral home."

"Can't afford it."

"The hospital's worse. It charges by the day."

"What in case I take his stuff and leave."

"The county'll bury him."

"That'll run you how much?"

"About a thousand."

"That's a lot of money."

The sheriff nodded.

"Tell you what," Gerald said. "I'll sell you his car for one dollar. You can use it to pay off what all he owes. There's that radio and stuff. Plus I'll throw in a hundred cash."

"You can't buy a body."

"It ain't yours to sell or mine to buy. I just want to get him home. Family wants him."

"I don't know if it's legal."

"He ain't the first person to die somewhere else. My cousin's aunt came in on a train after getting killed in a wreck. They set her off at the Rocksalt station. She was in a box."

The sheriff puffed his cheeks and blew air. He went to his office and dialed the courthouse and asked for a notary public. Half an hour later the car belonged to the city of Wahoo. It was a Chevelle and for a moment Gerald wondered if he'd made a mistake. They were pretty good cars.

The sheriff drove them to the hospital. Gerald pulled the money out and started counting.

"Keep it," the sheriff said.

"Give it to Melanie. She wants menthol cigarettes."

"You and Ory aren't a whole lot alike, are you."

"I never knew him that good."

"The only man I saw give money away was my daddy."

"Was he rich?"

"No," said the sheriff, "Daddy was a farmer."

"You all worked this flat land?"

"It worked him right back into it."

Gerald followed the sheriff into the hospital and signed several forms. An orderly wheeled in a gurney with the body on it, covered with a white cloth. He pushed it to an exit beside the emergency room. Three ambulances drove into the lot and paramedics began moving the injured people into the hospital. The orderlies left the gurney and went to help. A state police car stopped behind the ambulances.

"I have to talk to them," the sheriff said. "Then I'll get an ambulance to drop the body down at the train station."

The sheriff left the car and walked to the state trooper. Nobody was looking at Gerald. He pushed the gurney into the lot and along the side of the building. A breeze rippled the cloth that covered Ory. Gerald held it down with one hand but the gurney went crooked. He let go of the cloth and righted the gurney and the wind blew the cloth away. Ory was stretched out naked with a hole in his side. He didn't look dead, but Gerald didn't think he looked too good either. He looked like a man with a bad hangover that he might shake by dinner.

Gerald dropped the tailgate of his pickup and dragged Ory into the truck. He threw his blanket over him and weighted the corners with tire tools, the spare, and a coal shovel. He drove the rest of the day. In Illinois, he stopped and lay down beside the truck. Without the blanket he was cold, but he didn't feel right about taking it back from Ory. Gerald thought about Ory asking Melanie to wear the blond wig. He wondered if it made a difference when they were in bed.

He woke with frost on him. A buzzard circled high above the truck. He drove into the rising sun, thinking that he'd done everything backward. No matter when he drove, he was always aimed at the sun. Mist lifted above the land as the frost gave way. At the next exit, Gerald left the interstate for a farm road and parked beside a plowed field.

He carried the shovel over a wire fence. The dirt was loose and easy to take. It would make a fine garden at home. His body took over, grateful for the labor after three days of driving. A pair of redwing blackbirds sat on a power line, courting each other, and Gerald wondered how birds knew to go with their own kind. Maybe Ory knew he was in the wrong tree and that's why he wanted Melanie to wear a wig. Gerald tried to imagine her with blond hair. He suddenly understood that he wanted her, had wanted her at the jailhouse. He couldn't figure why. It bothered him that he had so much desire for a woman he didn't consider attractive.

He climbed in the back and mounded the dirt to balance the load. As he traveled south, he reentered spring. The buds of softwood trees turned pale green. Flocks of starlings moved over him in a dark cloud, heading north. By nightfall, he crossed the Ohio River into Kentucky. In four hours he'd be home. He was getting sleepy, but coffee had stopped doing him any good. He slid into a zone of the road, letting the rhythm of motion enter his body. A loud noise made him jerk upright. He thought he'd had a flat until he saw that he'd drifted across the breakdown lane and onto the edge of the median. He parked and lay down in the bench seat. He was lucky not to have been killed. The law would have a hard time with that—two dead men, one naked and already stiff, and a load of dirt.

When he woke, it was light and he felt tired already. At a gas station he stared at the rest room mirror, thinking that he looked like the third day of a three-day drunk. The suit was ruined. He combed his hair with water and stepped into the sun. A dog was in the back of his pickup, digging. Gerald yelled, looking for something to grab. The dog saw him and jumped off the truck and loped away. Gerald shoved dirt over Ory's exposed hand. A man came behind him.

"Shoo-eee," the man said. "You waited long enough didn't you."

Gerald grunted. He was smoothing the dirt, re-
placing the weights along the blanket's edge. The
man spoke again.

"Had to take one to the renderers myself last
week. Got some kind of bug that killed it in three
days. Vet said it was a new one on him."

"A new one."

"I put mine in a garbage bag. Keeps the smell in
better than dirt."

"It does."

"Did yours up and not eat, then lay down and
start breathing hard?"

"More or less."

"It's the same thing. A malady, the vet called it."

"A malady."

Gerald got in the truck and decided not to stop
until he was home. The stench was bad and getting
worse. He wondered if breathing a bad smell made
your lungs stink. The land started to roll, the crests
rising higher as he traveled east. The sun was very
hot. It seemed to him as if summer had arrived
while he was gone. He'd been to winter and back.

Deep in the hills, he left the interstate for a black-
top road that turned to dirt, following the twists of a

creek. He stopped at the foot of his wife's home hill. Kay would be up there, at her mom's house with all her family. They would feed him, give him whiskey, wait for him to tell what happened. He brushed off his suit and thought about the events, collecting them in sequence. He told the story in his head. He thought some more, then practiced again. Ory had quit drinking and taken a good job as manager of a department store. He'd gotten engaged to a woman he'd met at church, but had held off telling the family until he could bring her home. She was nice as pie, blond headed. He was teaching her to shoot a pistol and it went off by accident. She was tore all to pieces about it. He'd never seen anyone in such bad shape. All she did was cry. It was a malady.

Gerald drove slowly up the hill. Later, he could tell the truth to the oldest brother, who'd tell the rest. They'd appreciate his public lie and he'd be in with the family. He parked in the yard beside his mother-in-law's house. Dogs ran toward the truck, then kids. Adults stepped onto the porch and Gerald could see them looking for Ory in the cab. Kay came out of the house. She smiled at him, the same small smile that she always used, and he wondered how she'd look in a wig.

He got out of the truck and waited. Everything was the same—the house, the trees, the people. He recognized the leaves and the outline of the branches against the sky. He knew how the light would fall, where the shadows would go. The smell of the woods was familiar. It would be this way for-ever. Abruptly, as if doused by water, he knew why Ory had left.

Melungeons

Deputy Goins sat in his office and watched the light that seeped beneath the door of the jailhouse. When it reached a certain pock in the floor, it would be time to go home. Monday was nearly over. In the town of Rocksalt, the deputy doubled as jailer to balance each job's meager pay. Goins had come in early to free his prisoners in time for work at the sawmill. They'd left laughing, three boys who'd gotten drunk through the weekend. Goins had spent all day in the dim office. He was tired.

Something outside blocked the light and Goins

wished the county would buy a clock. A man opened the door.

"Time is it?" Goins said.

The man shrugged. He peered into the dark room, jerking his head like a blackbird on a fence rail. He looked older than Goins, who was sixty-three, and Goins thought he'd probably come for a grandson.

"Nobody here," Goins said. "Done turned them loose."

"I heard tell a Goins worked here."

"That's me. Ephraim Goins."

"Well, I'm fit for the pokey. What's a man got to do to go?"

"Drunk mostly."

"Don't drink."

"Speeding."

"Ain't got nary a car."

"Stealing'll do it."

"I don't reckon."

The man kept his head turned and his eyes down. Goins decided that he was a chucklehead who'd wandered away from his family.

"Why don't you let me call your kin," Goins said.

"No phone." The man jerked his chin to the corridor where the cells were. "What if I cussed you?"

"I'd cuss back."

"Ain't they nothing?"

"Let's see," Goins said. "Defacing public property is on the books, but it'd be hard to hurt this place."

The man walked to the door and stood with his back turned. "Come here a minute," he said.

Goins joined him. The man had unzipped his pants and was urinating on the plank steps leading to the door. Goins whistled low, shaking his head.

"You've force put me, sure enough," he said, hoping to scare the man away. "Looks like you're arrested. Lucky they ain't no lynch mob handy."

The man inhaled deeply and hurried down the hall to a cell. Goins opened the heavy door. The man stepped in and quickly pulled it shut behind him.

"Name?" said Goins.

"Gipson. Haze Gipson."

He lifted his head, showing blue eyes in rough

contrast with his black hair and smooth, swarthy skin. They watched each other for a long time. The name Gipson was like Goins, a Melungeon name, and Goins knew the man's home ridge deep in the hills. He glanced along the dim hall and lowered his voice.

"Say you're a Gipson?"

"Least I ain't the law."

"What's your why of getting locked up?"

"You been towned so long," Gipson said, "I don't know that I can say. I surely don't."

"Why not?"

"Don't know which way you're aimed at these days."

Goins stepped close to the bars.

"You know," he said. "If you're a Gipson, you do. But you ain't making it easy."

"It never was."

Gipson lay on the narrow cot and rolled on his side, turning his back to Goins. A mouse blurred across the floor.

"I'm a done-talk man," Gipson said.

Goins returned to his desk. He stared through the window at the courthouse and remembered his fourth-grade teacher threatening a child who was always late to school. "If you don't get up on time," the teacher had said, "the Melungeons will get you." Melungeons weren't white, black, or Indian. They lived deep in the hills, on the most isolated ridges, pushed from the hollows two centuries back by the people following Boone. The Shawnee called them "white Indians," and told the settlers that they'd always lived there. Melungeons continued to live as they always had.

Goins wasn't born when the trouble started between the Gipson and Mullins clans, but he'd felt the strain of its tension all his life. Members of his family had married both sides. To avoid the pressure of laying claim to either, Goins had volunteered to serve in Korea. Uniforms rather than blood would clarify the enemy.

When a dentist noticed that his gums were tinged with blue, the army assigned Goins to an all-black company. Black soldiers treated him with open scorn. The whites refused to acknowledge him at all. Only one man befriended him, a New Yorker named Abe, whom no one liked because he was Jewish.

On a routine patrol Goins became separated from the rest, and was not missed until the sound of gunfire. American soldiers found him bleeding from two bullet holes and a bayonet wound. Five enemy lay dead around him. Goins was decorated with honor and returned to Kentucky, but stayed in town. He didn't want to live near killing. Out of respect for its only hero, the town overlooked which hill he was from. Now the town had forgotten.

Goins rose from his desk and walked to Gipson's cell, his boots echoing in the dark hall. The smell of human waste and disinfectant made his nose sting. The walls were damp.

"How long you aim to stay?" Goins said.

"Just overnight. Hotel's too risky."

"Why stay in town at all?"

"Man gets old," Gipson said. "You don't know who I am, do you?"

"No," Goins said. "I ain't been up there in thirty years."

"Longer for me. I'm the one that left and went north."

"Plenty of work?"

"As many taxes they got laying for a man, it don't hardly pay to work."

"What'd they take you for up there?"

"Went by ever who else was around. Italian mostly. Couple times a Puerto Rican till they heard me talk. Sometimes it never mattered."

"Why come back?"

"I got give out on it," Gipson said. "I'm seventy-six years old. Missed every wedding and funeral my family had."

"Me, too."

"By choice." The man's voice was hard. "You can walk back out your ridge any day of the year. Don't know why a man wouldn't when he could."

Goins gripped the cell door with both hands the way prisoners often stood, shoulders hunched, head low. He didn't hunt or fish anymore, had stopped gathering mushrooms and ginseng. Being in the woods was too painful when he didn't live there. The last few times he'd felt awkward and foreign, as if the land was mocking him. He wondered if Gipson's exile was easier without the constant reminder of what he'd lost.

Goins unlocked the cell and pulled the door open
an inch. Gipson's face twisted in a faint smile. One
side of his mouth was missing teeth.

"I'm going," said Goins.

"I'll be here come daylight."

"Hope you know what you're doing."

"Some of my grandkids have got kids," Gipson
said. "You don't know what it's like to see them all
at once. And them not to know you."

"You were up to the mountain?" Goins said.

The man nodded.

"Bad as ever?"

"Not so much as it was. They're married in now
and don't bother with it no more. The kids have got
a game of it, play-acting. I look for it to stop when
the next bunch gets born. Still ain't full safe for me.
I'm the last of the old Gipsons left alive."

He moved to face the wall again. Goins walked
quietly away, leaving the cell open, hoping Gipson
would change his mind. He left the front door unlocked. The dusk of autumn cooled his face and he
realized that he'd been sweating. The fading sun
leaned into the hills with a horizontal light that
made the woods appear on fire.

• • •

A gibbous moon waned above the land when Beulah Mullins left her house. Though she hadn't been off the mountain in fifty years, she found the old path easily, and followed it down the final slanting drop to the road beside the creek. The road was black now, hard and black. She'd heard of that but never seen it. Beulah stayed on the weedy shoulder, preferring earth for the long walk to Rocksalt. The load she carried was easier on flat terrain.

Beulah had never voted or paid taxes. There was no record of her birth. The only time she'd been to town, she'd bought nails for a hogpen. Her family usually burned old buildings for nails, plucking them hot from the debris, but that year a spring flood had washed them away. Beulah had despised Rocksalt and swore never to return. Tonight she had no choice. She left her house within an hour of learning that Haze was on the mountain. He'd slipped away, probably after hearing that she was still alive, and headed for town. Beulah walked steadily. The air was day-white from the moon.

Sixty years before, five Mullins men were logging a hillside at the southern edge of their property when a white oak slipped sideways from its notch. The beveled point dug into the earth. Instead of falling parallel with the creek, the oak dropped onto their neighbor's land and splintered a hollow log. Dislodged tree leaves floated in the breeze. When the men crossed the creek, they found a black bear crushed to death inside the hollow log. They built a fire for the night and ate the liver, tongue, and six pounds of greasy fat.

In the morning, a hunting party of Gipsons discovered the camp. The land was theirs and they demanded the meat. Since the Mullins men had already butchered the bear, they offered half. The Gipsons refused. Three men died in a quick gunfight. The rest crept through the woods, leaking blood from bullet wounds. Over the next two decades, twenty-eight more people were killed, a few per year.

Ground fog rose to the eastern sky, streaked in pink like lace. Beulah's face was dark as a ripe pawpaw. Checkered gingham wrapped her head, covering five feet of grey hair. She wore a long coat that smelled of oil and concealed her burden. Her legs hurt. A flock of vireos lifted from a maple by the creek, a thick cloud of dark specks that narrowed at the end like a tadpole. Beulah watched them, knowing that winter would arrive early.

She scented town before she saw the buildings. Rocksalt was bigger now, had spread like moss. Frost in the hills was heavy enough to track a rabbit, but here the ground was soft. Town was suddenly all around her. Beulah moved downwind of a police car. She couldn't read, but knew that an automobile with writing on its side was like a tied dog. Whoever held the leash controlled it. She stalked the town from the shade. Her shins were damp from dew.

Railroad Street was empty. The muddy boardwalk was gone, and the cement sidewalk reminded her of a frozen creek, shiny and hard in the shade. Beulah leaned against the granite whistle post in the morning sun. On her last trip this had been the center of town, busy with people, wagons, and mules. Now the tracks were rusty and the platform was a bare gantry of rotted wood. Beulah looked past it to the tree line, listening to a cardinal. The hollow was glazed by mist like crystal.

She turned her back and headed into the silence

of improvement. Sunlight crept down the buildings that faced east. She walked two blocks out of her way to avoid a neon diner sign glowing in the dawn. No one here would take Haze in. There was only one place he could have gone.

A bench sat in front of the jail with one side propped on a concrete block. The load she carried prevented her from sitting and she moved to shade, leaning against the southern wall. She was eighty-four years old. She breathed easily in the chill air.

Goins slept rough that night, listening to the building crack from overnight cold. At dawn he rose and looked at the hills. He missed living with the land most in autumn, when the trees seemed suddenly splashed in color, and rutting deer snorted in the hollows. There were walnuts to gather, bees to rob. Turkeys big as dogs jumped from ridgelines to extend their flight.

He rubbed his face and turned from the window, reminding himself of why he'd stayed in Rocksalt. Town was warm. It had cable TV and water. He was treated as everyone's equal, but his years in town had taught him to hide his directness, the Melungeon way of point-blank living.

After breakfast, he reached under his bed for a cigar box that contained his Purple Heart and Bronze Star. They were tarnished near to black. Beneath them was an article he'd cut from a Lexington paper a few years back. It was a feature story suggesting that Melungeons were descendants of Madoc, a Welsh explorer in the twelfth century. Alternate theories labeled them as shipwrecked Portuguese, Phoenicians, Turks, or one of Israel's lost tribes. It was the only information Goins had ever seen about Melungeons. The article called them a vanishing race.

He slipped the brittle paper in his pocket and walked to work. Strands of mist haloed the hills that circled the town. The jailhouse door was unlocked, and Goins hoped the cell would be empty.

Inside, Gipson sat silently on his bunk, making a cigarette. Goins gave him a cup of coffee. The cigarette hung from Gipson's mouth. Once lit, he never touched it.

"Sleep good?" Goins said.

"My back hurts like a toothache."

Goins unfolded the newspaper article and handed it through the bars. Gipson read it slowly.

"Don't mean nothing," he said. "They're just fighting over who come to America first. Damn sure wasn't you and me."

"I kindly favor that lost tribe of Israel idea."

"You do."

"I've give thought to it. Them people then moved around more than a cat. Your name's off Hezekiah and mine's Ephraim. I knowed a Nimrod once. Got a cousin Zephaniah married a Ruth."

Gipson shook his head rapidly, sending a trail of ash to the grimy floor.

"That don't make us nobody special," he said.

"We're somebody, ain't we."

"We damn sure ain't Phoenicians or Welshes. We ain't even Melungeons except in the paper. It don't matter where we upped from. It's who we are now that matters."

"Man can study on it if he's a mind to."

"You're a Goins."

"I'm a deputy."

Goins returned to his desk. He wanted to ask for

the article back but decided to wait until the man wasn't twitchy as a spooked horse. A preacher had donated a Bible for the prisoners and Goins hunted through Genesis for his namesake, the leader of a lost tribe who never made it to the land of milk and honey. He hoped it was hilly. He turned to Exodus and thought of Abe, his army buddy from New York. Goins wondered if he had a phone. Maybe Abe knew where the lost tribes went.

The jail's front door slowly creaked open and a woman's form eclipsed the light that flowed around her. She stepped inside. Goins didn't know her, but he knew her. It was as if the mountain itself had entered the tiny room, filling it with earth and rain, the steady wind along the ridge. She gazed at him, one eye dark, the other yellow-flecked. Between the lines of her face ran many smaller lines like rain gulleys running to creeks. She'd been old when he was young.

"You look a Goins," she said.

He nodded. He could smell the mountain on her.

"They a Gipson here?" she said.

Goins nodded again. He swallowed in order to speak, but couldn't.

The woman shifted her shoulders to remove a game bag. Inside was a blackened pot, the lid fastened with moonseed vine. She looked at him, waiting. He opened a drawer for a plate and she removed the lid to reveal a skin of grease that covered a stew. She scooped a squirrel leg onto his plate, then a potato. The musk of fresh game pushed into the room. Her hands were misshapen from arthritis but she used them freely, her lips clamped tight. Goins understood that she was following the old code of proving the pot contained no file or pistol. He relaxed some. She wasn't here for trouble.

The woman shifted her head to look at him. The blink of her eyes was slow and patient. She stood as if she could wait a month without speech or movement, oblivious to time and weather. Goins tried again to speak. He wanted to ask her where they'd all come from, but knew from looking at her that she wouldn't know or care.

When he realized what she was waiting for, he opened his pocketknife, sliced some meat from the leg, and lifted it to his mouth. It tasted of wild onion and the dark flavor of game. He nodded to her. She straightened her back and faced the hall and did not look at him again.

She walked to the cells, moving stiffly, favoring her left side as if straining with gout. The long coat rustled against her legs like brush in a breeze. Goins pivoted in his chair to give them privacy. He looked at the strip of light below the front door, knowing that as the sun passed by, the light would get longer, then shorter, before he could leave. Outside, someone laughed while entering the courthouse. A car engine drowned the sound of morning birds. Goins stared at the closed door. He swallowed the bite of meat.

Behind him he heard the woman say one word soaked in the fury of half a century. Then came the tremendous bellow of a shotgun. The sound bounced off the stone walls and up the hall to his office, echoing back and forth, until it faded. Goins jerked upright in the chair. His legs began to shiver. He held his thighs tightly and the shivering traveled up his arms until his entire body shook. He pressed his forehead against the desk. When the trembling passed, he went down the hall to the cells.

Gun smoke stung his eyes and he could smell

cordite. The left side of the woman's coat was hiked across her hip where she'd hidden the gun. Its barrel was shiny and ragged at the sawcut. Her legs were steady. She tossed the weapon into the cell, looked at Goins and nodded once, her expression the same as before.

The cigarette in Gipson's cell still trailed smoke. Blood covered the newspaper article and flowed slowly across the floor. The woman stepped to the next cell and waited while he unlocked the door. Her face seemed softer. She stepped inside. When the door clanked shut, her back stiffened, and she lifted her head to the gridded square of sky visible through the small window.

People were running outside. Someone shouted his name, asking if he was hurt. Goins used the phone to call an undertaker who doubled as county coroner. It occurred to him that coroner was a better job than jailer. The coroner would receive twenty-five dollars for pronouncing the man dead, but Goins got nothing extra for cleaning the cell.

He put the Bible away and found the prisoner's log and wrote Mullins. Under yesterday's date he wrote Gipson. Goins rubbed his eyes. He didn't write Haze because the man was down to a body now, and the body was a Melungeon. Goins covered his face with his hands. It was true for him as well. He opened the door and stepped into the sun. People ducked for cover until they recognized him. He looked at them, men and women he'd known for thirty years, but never really knew. Beyond them stood the hills that hemmed the town. He began walking east, toward the nearest slope. There was nothing he needed to take. The sun was warm against his face.

Moscow, Idaho

Tilden stopped digging and wiped his sleeve across his forehead, leaving a brown smear on his skin. The afternoon sunlight shimmered in the air. He jabbed the shovel into the ground. His arms were sore and his back hurt, but anything was better than prison, even moving graves in Idaho.

The cemetery sat on a rise outside of town, surrounded by wheat fields that were ready for harvest. The grain rose high and golden, swaying in the wind. Next spring the state was building a highway through the cemetery. Tilden and a fellow ex-con named Baker had spent the last few weeks unearthing coffins. They'd been hired to replace a mini backhoe that damaged the caskets, sometimes cutting them in half. A separate work crew hauled the coffins to the other side of Moscow for reburial.

September still had some hard heat and the two men moved to the lacy shade of a tamarack. Sweat evaporated from their skin. Baker reached into his shirt pocket for a cigarette without removing the pack. Tilden recognized the prison habit and wondered what traits he still carried.

"You know," Baker said, "back in Minnesota they got the biggest mall in the world."

Tilden nodded. Baker liked to talk and needed periodic proof that someone was paying attention.

"There's six bars in that mall," Baker said, "and nothing but rent-a-cops. You can get drunk and walk from one bar to another and nobody fucks with you. Not bad, huh?"

Tilden nodded.

"I ever tell you the best thing about getting locked up in St. Paul?" Baker said.

"The view."

"That's right, partner. The river was right there.

You could watch boats all day from my cell. Bet you didn't have no view in Kentucky, did you?"

Tilden had been among the first prisoners assigned to a new facility in Morgan County. People called it the Pink Palace due to the pastel color of its outer walls. The prison was surrounded by hills. Sometimes groundfog prevented the men from going into the yard because the sharpshooter in the tower couldn't see well enough. On clear mornings, each tree leaf was distinct in the mountain light. Their presence was a tease, like a friend's wife who liked to flirt.

Tilden wondered if a view of the river made men sadder or gave them hope. He figured the prison psychologist would like it, since he favored anything that was different, even a new coat of paint. Tilden had learned to give the shrink what he wanted, which was mainly the impression that you wouldn't shank the first son of a bitch who looked at you mad dog. Getting through the joint took the ability to make everyone think you were crazy enough to be dangerous. Getting out was the opposite. Tilden wasn't sure what it took to stay out.

Heat was on him like water, pressing against his sunburnt face. He and Baker took a break on the shadowed side of a stand of pine. The oldest tombstones were pale with black stains, the lettering nearly worn away. Faded plastic flowers surrounded the newer stones. Beyond them lay fresh earth waiting for the dead.

"You know something," Baker said. "I ain't spent a whole lot of time in a graveyard."

"Reckon not."

"I was just a kid last time, for my grandmaw's funeral. I ever tell you about her?"

"No."

"She died."

"I guessed that."

"Hung herself from a clothes pole in a closet. Knocked her own wheelchair out from under her. The only suicide the nursing home said they ever had, but you can't trust them bastards."

"You got that right."

"They ought to lock that home down. A little blue-haired lady with no legs hanging in a closet like an old dress."

"No legs?"

"She had diabetes," Baker said. "Know what they did so nobody else would do it?"

"Threw them in the hole."

"No, man. They took away the clothes pole in every closet. They can't hang nothing no more. All them old folks wearing wrinkly clothes. Just like Deer Lodge. We had a man shoot somebody in the belly with a staple gun he'd rigged to fire a home-made bullet. He'd stole it from Art and they shut down Art tight as a fucking drum. It was my best class. I made pictures of the ocean. Ever see the ocean?"

"No."

"Me neither. That's why I made them pictures. Anyhow, my grandmaw got her gravesite picked out and paid for about a hundred years ago. It was waiting on her, but coffins got big over the years and there wasn't enough room. They had to dig up a whole row of my family to get her in there."

"Guess those others died too soon."

"Or her too late."

"I ain't knocking your grandmaw," Tilden said, "but I can't see owning a burial plot. It's the same as having your own cell in case you get put away."

"Hell, if I owned a grave, I'd have hocked it on jump street."

They laughed together, the sound fading in the still air. Tilden ate an apple while Baker smoked. Each tombstone threw a narrow shadow that lay over the adjacent grave like a puddle. According to the dates, many people had been dead longer than they had lived. Tilden knew men who'd spent more years in prison than out, and it occurred to him that time didn't move forward as he'd always thought. People moved through time instead.

"Ever miss the joint?" Baker said.

"I don't reckon."

"I do. The dope especially. I had good connections inside. Out here, I don't know nobody."

"Well, you best watch or that mandatory sentencing will eat you up. I celled with a guy did two murders and he was on the street before the dopers."

"I like that mandatory law," Baker said.

"Do you."

"You bet. Fill them cells up with hopheads and they ain't got room for you and me."

"They don't need room for me."

"Big talk," Baker said. "You know why they called me Storebought inside?"

Tilden nodded.

"My first beef. They popped me on some over-the-counter caffeine pills. I kept telling them it was storebought dope but you can't tell the law nothing."

"I hear that."

"Tell you what else I miss," Baker said. "All the different guys you meet. I thought it would be like high school and you went to whatever prison was close. I met guys inside nothing like home. They were from all over the country. Sometimes I miss those guys. I miss them calling me Storebought, too."

"I know what you mean."

"What I don't like about being out, I never had to hang in a graveyard before."

Tilden didn't miss anything about prison, but he could understand Baker's desire for routine. They ate lunch under the same ponderosa pines every day, and after work they went to the same bar. Baker was like a bee, needing to follow a pattern over and over. Prison was his hive. In custody, he flourished.

"Eight years in the can," Baker said. "TV was the biggest thing that changed."

"Some."

"I seen a guy on it saying you shouldn't eat eggs because raising chickens was slavery."

"Talking out his neck, ain't he."

"Only thing good are these true cop shows. They think they're bragging how great the police are, but all they really show is how the chumps get caught. A guy can learn something."

"Not exactly."

"I guess you're Square Johning on me."

"Aim to."

"Shouldn't be kicking it with me then."

"Way I see it," Tilden said, "maybe I'm a good influence on you."

"Best influence I ever had was inside. A fence told me what not to move, and a paperhanger said what to look for on funny money. Hell, even the government's doing me good with the gun laws. TV says they got people walking in off the street and giving their guns up. I, for one, am all for it. That's one less bullet to hit me on a job. Citizens are a bunch of morons. The government figured that out a million years ago."

"I never thought about it that way."

"Well, if you watched TV, you'd know something."

Gravestones rose like teeth from the earth. Tilden wondered how many people buried here had been killed by a bullet. Baker would no more blame a gun for somebody getting shot than he'd scapegoat a shovel for the graveyard. Laws would never slow him down. He didn't think far enough ahead and getting caught would never happen. There were thousands like him. Tilden wondered if he was lumping himself in with that group. He didn't think so, but he was an ex-con, working a job that no one else would take.

He threw a piece of apple to a squirrel. He'd prefer to feed the birds, but since the squirrels got it first, he went ahead and fed them. He considered it a lesson from prison—not trying to force what he wanted. Still, Tilden knew how the birds felt, compromised right out of the deal.

"You get anything else from being down?" he said.

"Muscles," Baker said. "I worked out every day. And my tats."

One forearm said FTW, and the other showed the number thirteen and a half. He unbuttoned his shirt and slid the collar over one shoulder to reveal a blurred tattoo. Two crudely drawn dice had snake eyes showing. Below them, in block letters, was the phrase BORN TO LOSE.

"No," Tilden said. "I mean anything worth keeping in your head."

"You talk like a shrink."

"Come on, man."

Baker cracked his knuckles one by one. He stretched his legs until his boots reached the last lip of shade. He stared into space and Tilden decided that he'd forgotten the question, led somewhere private by the skipping of his thoughts. He'd noticed that prison often made stupid men turn smart, and smart men become dumb. He wondered which he was.

Baker lay on his back and spoke.

"Biggest thing I learned is how to make people leave me alone. Next is how to sleep. I never slept good before, but now I can sleep fourteen hours."

"Nothing else?"

"I damn sure know I like women."

Passing clouds pushed patterns of shade along the ground. A breeze carried the scent of wheat mixing with the smell of fresh-turned earth. It occurred to Tilden that people always buried their dead on hilltops, often the highest around. Tilden liked the silence. Prison was filled with noise—the crash of steel gates, howls of rage and pain, blaring radios. The only quiet time came after homicide. Tilden had never seen murder until he got put away, and he'd been amazed at how fast it could happen.

Now he sat surrounded by dead that went back a hundred years. Tilden wondered how far into the earth he'd have to dig before he'd stop hitting bone. He understood that the planet was a skin of grass that covered acres of bone, like a skeleton for the earth. Dirt was sinew. Rock was muscle.

After the break they walked to a grave that had been tough to work. They'd dug two days, chopping through roots that veered around the coffin, sometimes holding it tight as if the earth wanted to keep the bones. Tilden was reminded of an old con who'd finally been cut loose. He'd done a twenty-five-year flat bit for a bank robbery that had earned him high status in prison. Outside, he was an old man no one cared about. Nine days into freedom he held up a bar, set his pistol on a stool, and called the police. He returned to prison smiling, glad to be home. A week later he was stabbed three times with a knife made from the instep support of a crippled con's shoe.

Footsteps pounded in the lane behind Tilden and he turned to the noise. A man was running toward him. He wore green jogging tights and a spandex shirt. Mirrorshades covered his eyes and an antenna bobbed above yellow headphones.

Baker lifted his shovel like a baseball bat. Tilden wanted to shout a warning to leave the man alone, but it went against yard ethics. The jogger came abreast and Baker fell in step behind him.

"Run!" he yelled. "Crank it up, punk."

The man doubled his pace, puffs of dust rising from his feet. He veered around a bend and disappeared among the pines. Baker grinned. There was a wild expression on his face that Tilden had seen only in prison.

"I was in that big a hurry," Baker said, "I'd by

God get me a car. See me doing that, you can drop me in a sack. Know what I'm saying?"

"I'll pass on that."

"I know you're standup, Til. But if I didn't, I might wonder what you're afraid of."

"I'm chicken of one thing."

"What's that?"

"Myself."

"You bet," Baker said. "I wouldn't mess with me if I was me."

"That ain't exactly what I meant."

Tilden began moving earth, thinking of the last time he'd seen Baker's look on someone's face. Two men had circled each other in the rec room, slashing with weapons made from a razor blade embedded in a toothbrush handle. Each man wore magazines strapped to his torso by strips of sheet. They bled from the arms, but the crude armor protected their bodies. The crowd drew guards who beat both men unconscious. Tilden had still been a new fish, so scared he couldn't sleep, stunned by the savagery of the guards. The look in their eyes had matched Baker's.

Tilden and Baker worked through the slanting

red light of afternoon, continuing until dusk. They carried their tools to the storage building. Ripe wheat gleamed as though the surface of the earth had caught fire. Nine cars were parked in the gravel lot reserved for a funeral party.

Tilden heard the neigh of a horse, and he and Baker followed the sound to a rise overlooking the cemetery's edge. A line of people followed a horse-drawn buckboard that held a coffin. Two of the men wore ill-fitting suits, but most were dressed in work clothes, boots, and hats. A few women wore black. Four children walked close together. The horse stopped beside a fresh hole and the men used straps to lift the coffin from the wagon and ease it into the grave.

"Look at that," Baker said. "Guess they don't know about the highway coming through."

"Maybe they already got the grave paid off."

"Long time since I was at a funeral," Baker said. "They wouldn't let me out when my mother died."

"That's tough."

"I never even seen her grave."

At the bottom of the hill a man was removing

shovels from the wagon. He passed them to each mourner as if handing out weapons. Tilden realized that the fresh earth would be easy to move.

"Hey, man," Baker said, "I ever tell you about a guard I knew on a firing squad in Utah."

"No."

"He said it was just a job, but I think he was fucked up. I mean, who'd want to live in Utah?"

"I don't know," Tilden said.

"Anyhow, you heard how one rifle is loaded with a blank so each man can think he wasn't the killer. Well, that's bullshit. There's no recoil from a blank so you know if you shot it. He said to make up for it, everybody aims away from the heart. Sometimes all five guys miss and the shot man flops around awhile. The day before, he gets to watch any video he wants."

The people in the funeral party were filling the grave with dirt. They worked slowly, as if reluctant to finish. A woman rested, leaning on the handle of her shovel.

"They could use some help," Baker said.

"I don't know about that."

"Why not?"

"If it was some stranger wanting to bury my family, I might think it was funny."

"What's funny is that damn horse. Think they're Amish or something?"

"They don't have them out here."

"They don't have a lot," Baker said. "You like it?"

"What, Idaho?"

"All of it, man. The whole West."

"Yeah, I like it."

"I don't. All this empty space, you know, makes me feel lonely."

"That's why I like it," Tilden said.

A small boy knelt beside the grave and began pushing dirt in the hole. He worked steadily, using his arms to move the soil. A man took his shoulders from behind. The boy shoved him away and began throwing the dirt faster. He lay on the ground with his arms dangling in the grave.

"Probably his mother," Tilden said.

Tears made clean lines in the dirt on Baker's face. His chest rose and fell, and he began to pant as if he had lost the mechanics of how to cry.

Tilden walked down the hill to the storage building. He knew he had to be careful. Baker was dangerous now that Tilden had seen him weak. Tilden drank from a spigot and cleaned the shovels, thinking of the funerals he'd missed in prison. Those days had been the worst.

Baker came over the hill, walking with the gait of a mainline con, moving slowly from the hips down, his shoulders swaying in a swagger.

"I'm done, man," Baker said.

"What?"

"I can't work that grave."

"That's all right," Tilden said. "I will."

"No, man. I'm done with all of it."

"You quitting?"

"I didn't bury my own mother and here I am digging up strangers."

Baker ducked along the row of cars until he found one with the keys in it. He eased the door open and checked the lights, the gas gauge, and the turn signals.

"Tell me if the brake lights work," he called. "I got to hurry. They'll be here in a minute."

Baker searched the car, talking fast.

"I tell you about my first juvie pop? Stole a car that ran out of gas. There was a bag of dope under the seat. I'm glad they closed that file at eighteen, man. Nobody knows how stupid I used to be."

He pulled a pair of work gloves from the backseat.

"You want these?" he said. "Too small for me."

"This ain't worth it."

"What is, man?"

Baker dropped the gloves on the ground and opened the trunk.

"They got a spare and a jack," he said. "My lucky day, right. Too bad they didn't leave a purse."

"You can still walk away."

"I want to see the ocean. Let's go, man. We can road dog it out of here."

"No way." Tilden used his yard voice, low and quick. "I'm never going back inside."

"Me neither, man. I been down twice. I'll kill everybody up before they put me back in the walls. Everybody."

Tilden looked over the car's roof to the wheat field in the east. He couldn't find the seam where earth and sky blended together. The world was blurred by dusk.

"Don't keep this rig too long," Tilden said.

"I won't. Radio ain't got but AM anyhow."

"Later, Storebought."

Baker grinned at his nickname and drove away. Tilden left the cemetery quickly, before the funeral party returned to the lot. He knew what Baker was up to and where he was headed. He was on a run, like riding a motorcycle wide open until he crashed. The state called it recidivism, but as the old cons said, Baker was doing life on the installment plan.

Tilden crossed the road and lay on his back beside the wheat. He spread his arms. Wind blew loose dirt over his body. The ground was soft, and the air was warm. In prison he had figured out that laws were made to protect the people who made the laws. He had always thought that staying out of trouble meant following those laws, but now he knew there was more. The secret was to act like the people who wanted the laws in the first place. They didn't even think about it. They just lived.

Tilden wondered if he'd ever find a woman, a job he liked, or a town he wanted to stay in. Above him the Milky Way made a blizzard of stars in the sky. There was not a fence or wall in sight.

Two-Eleven All Around

When she locked me out I didn't mind that much because things were drifty from the start. She didn't like my drinking and I did not go for her Prozac and police scanner. Her kid was a pain in the ass, too. As much as I tried to get along with him, he was already what he always would be—a sullen little punk who liked the couch.

What happened was I came home drunk and she wouldn't let me in. She didn't even answer the door. It was night and I thought I was doing good by coming home before the bars closed, but it didn't matter to her. She's from right here in Casper, and they are

a tough people. She sat hunched over her police
scanner, not moving an inch. You'd think she was
dead but I knew what was going on. She'd got on her
high horse and was riding out a sober binge on anti-
depressants. She did this the same way other folks
went on vitamins and health food, sort of a home-
grown detox. I could hear static on the scanner, a
steady sound like fast water until she squelched it
and strangers spoke into the house.

At one time I tried to get into it, being a scanner-
head, thinking it was something we could share outside of drinking, fighting, and sex. I even memorized
part of the ten-code, what cops use on the radio. I
never understood why they talk in code, though. A
guide to it comes with the scanner, so it's not like
they're fooling anybody. And saying ten-four instead of okay does not exactly save time in a crucial
situation. My favorite was two-eleven all around,
which meant that the subject was clean, with no warrants against him in the city or county. The lucky
guy was free to go.

Nothing me and her did together was right except in the boinking department. It's not like she
had a great body or nothing, just average, but it was

attitude more than anything else. She'd do whatever came down the pike and not feel guilty later.
Me, I'm all for kinky sex, but sometimes thinking
about it is better than the doing. My best is in the afternoon, doing it regular while thinking about the
weird stuff.

Funny thing about that scanner, though, it
sucked her away from sex like getting religion.
She'd sit froze over it for hours, patched into a
world of good guys and bad guys, like a video game
except they were real. You hear the dispatcher call a
cruiser with an address, and after a few minutes the
cop says he's there. Then you sit and wait until the
cop comes on the air with the subject's name and
checks for outstanding warrants. Weekends were
busy, especially on a full moon, just like us and sex
in the old days.

Every few months, she'll go on Prozac, coffee,
and the scanner, then get mad if I got hammered. It
wasn't really fair but I understood she had to take
time off from drinking, because when she was on
safari, you better keep bail money handy. I could tell
what she'd been up to the night before by the dents
on the car. One thing, though, she didn't wake up

with the regrets. She never called around to see if she did anything she should apologize for. To me, that made her a full-blown alcoholic while I was just a drunk.

The Prozac always made her lose weight. She looked great but couldn't have an orgasm. She said it was the Prozac that did it, but since she was on it, she didn't mind. It bothered me a lot. It got so bad I was jealous of that scanner. Jealous of men who would never touch her. Jealous of voices in the dark.

She never gave me a reason to feel that way. It was my trip, not hers, and it went right to my father. He never drank a drop. He always held a job, and he lived in the same place all his life. What he did, though, was tomcat around with a different woman every day of the week. He made me cover for him when he slipped off to see his Tuesday girlfriend. Then on Wednesday he'd go bowling out of the county. Thursday he'd see a widow in town. He lived like a rabbit mostly, and you might say I had a few moms. These days I'm as loyal as bark to a tree.

Early on I asked her how many men she'd been

with before me, and let me tell you, it's the stupidest damn thing you can ask a girlfriend. I know that, but I did it anyway. I'm the kind of guy who'll do the stupidest damn thing at the worst time. If a guy's got no nose, I'll tell him he's lucky his eyes are good, because he damn sure can't wear glasses. Sometimes I'm surprised I ain't got shot yet. I always figured that's how I'd go, killed at night by a stranger. Casper is that kind of town.

She didn't say anything for a long while. There's a time period when you can tell that people are making up a lie, but hers stretched on so long, I knew the truth was coming. Then it hit me that she was maybe counting up, and that number was something I did not want to hear. I wanted to shift to another channel. Just squelch her answer and move to someone else's life.

Finally she looked at me and said, "What year?"

Well, that took the wind out of my sails, like getting kicked in the grazoint. And right there was where she was at—you ask a direct question and she'd answer with a question. She'd have made a great spy. She never gave a thing up. You could ask her if it was raining and she'd say, "Outside?" then not understand why I'd fly off the handle. We mainly lived at the top of our voices, even in the sackeroo.

The night she locked me out, I hid in the dark, watching her in the house. She's a big-boned woman who got pregnant young, quit school, and works as a waitress. Never got a nickel of child support. I guess you could say the breaks went against her, and getting mixed up with me might be one of those breaks.

Sometimes I watched her kid, which was easy because all he did was play video games. I couldn't get him to throw a baseball or football. When I was a kid, my father wouldn't do anything with me and now this boy wouldn't either. Sometimes I wondered if she was just using me to baby-sit, but I don't think so, no more than I used her place to sleep. Her kid wasn't that bad. He went to school, cooked for himself, and listened to his mother. He despised me, and who could blame him. I was just another stranger roaming his house and sleeping with his mom. I was the enemy.

I stayed on the porch until I got sick of listening to the scanner's static. The house just sat there, dark and hard and locked. It was her house. Everything in it belonged to her, even her kid. My own boy was two thousand miles away, back home in Kentucky. The way it works anymore is you don't raise your own kids. You raise someone else's while a stranger takes care of yours, and then when that doesn't work out, everyone moves along to the next person with a kid. It's like two assembly lines moving in opposite directions. At the end are grown kids who haven't been raised so much as jerked up.

You come to expect dealing with ex-husbands who don't like you and kids who know full well you ain't their real daddy. And you know your kid's going through the same damn thing. Right now there's some somebody living with my ex and wishing my son was out of the picture. That's why I'm nice to the kids of women I meet. It works out in the long run, and maybe someone'll be nice to my boy. He's fourteen and smart. He can be anything he wants to be.

The bars were closed and I walked an hour. I was between drunk and sober, which makes your mind go strange ways. At thirty-five years old, I was out of work with no place to sleep. Sometimes I don't think I've done anything to leave my mark in this world. I'm the kind of person the world leaves a mark on.

A patrol car cruised me but I stayed cool, and the cop probably made me for what I was—another poor bastard tossed out by his old lady. The second time he passed, he didn't even slow down, and an idea hit me like a ton of bricks.

I cut down a few streets to an old industrial building that was getting renovated into an espresso joint. There was rubble lying in the street that looked like giant bread crumbs. I picked up a chunk and stood there a long time, thinking everything through, then I tossed it in a slow underhand arc through the plate glass window. It made a beautiful sound that rang along the empty street like music.

I leaned against a lightpole and waited. There was a grin on my face you couldn't wipe off with a chain saw because I knew the police would come and ask for my I.D. And I knew she'd hear it all. She'd hear the cop read my last name and ask for a 10-29, which means check for wanteds. A minute would go by and the dispatcher would say, "Subject is two-eleven all around." And she damn sure knew the truth of that. I wasn't wanted anywhere, city or county, not even at home.

The cruiser came down the street, the candy rack on top flashing, no siren. I stepped away from the pole and held my arms away from my body and the cop put a light on me like a poacher jacklighting a deer. There was no sound but my breath. The door opened and the cop came toward me, walking slowly in case I was hopped up on crank. I stood there waiting in that streetlight's glare with broken glass at my back and garbage at my feet and the whole galaxy over my head, and suddenly I knew damn sure what would happen one day.

I'll have my own place and a job. It'll be late at night and I'll be asleep. Someone starts banging at the door. I stagger over in my underwear and open the door and there's a stranger standing there, two or three strangers. Behind them in the street is an old shitbox out of Detroit, jacked up in the back. These punks are outside my door with patches of hair on their young faces, wearing boots and sleeveless shirts to show their tattoos. I face them with my beer belly and think that even though I live alone in a little dump, dirty and cramped, it's still my damn place, and I'm willing to go down defending it. It's all I've got and it's not even really mine, just a rental, but I live here. You don't mess with a man in his own place.

I stand there in the night and look at these criminals, because that's what they are—there's nothing two-eleven about them. The street is empty and I'm alone. I don't want to show how twitchy I am on the inside so I say, "What the fuck do you want?"

And one looks at the rest with a sneer, and says, "See, I told you." Then he looks at me and says, "We're just hunting a place to flop, Dad."

It hits me who I'm looking at, a ripping that starts in my throat and runs to the soles of my feet. I can barely breathe. I hold onto the doorjamb to stay steady while I stare at this boy.

There's a part of me that wants to say, "Get a look, son. Burn this in your brain, boy. See the grime along the molding? See the empty beer cans with cigarette ashes around the holes? See the beat-up furniture and the dirty sheets? Take a good look, son. Take a picture because this is where you'll wind up at, and you don't want it. You do not want this."

But I don't say it. I never gave him anything before. And now I can't even give him this.

Instead, I open the door wide.

High Water Everywhere

Zules drove slowly, the headlights of his eighteen-wheeler dull against the fog. He'd driven in rain for two days, and it was hard to know where the road left off and the land began. The moon and stars were gone. He was running heavy through Oregon, following the Lower Callapooya River to avoid weigh stations on the interstate.

Over the trucker's channel came a report that a dike had broken. Zules switched to the local police band and heard a cop's voice telling emergency workers to evacuate immediately. The river wasn't just spilling over the top of the dike. Pressure had torn a hole through a weak spot and water was surging across the bottomland.

Zules steered to the shoulder and stepped out of the truck. Blown rain stung his face and arms. He cranked down the trailer legs and unscrewed the hoses that held the brake and electric lines. He worked fast, smashing a finger in the darkness, paying no more attention than if he'd nicked the handle of a tool. He didn't feel right about leaving his load, but without its extra weight he could beat the coming water. He climbed into his truck and pushed hard through the gears. The land reminded him of a tabletop, and he was heading for its edge.

When he reached a roadblock manned by a state trooper, he knew he'd outrun the river gushing through the dike. Zules slipped his hand into his shirt pocket and touched the small gourd his mother had given him for luck. It was dry.

He drove to Crawfordsville, got a room, and reported his abandoned trailer to the county sheriff. Zules was so tired he was wide awake. At the motel lounge he ordered bourbon and branch. The only customer was a woman slumped at the bar with her eyes closed, both hands around an empty glass. She lifted her head.

"Don't mean to bother you," Zules said.

"You didn't," she said. "I was just testing my eyelids for light leaks."

Zules told her about losing his trailer. She listened as if his story were common. Her clothes were wet and muddy.

"It rained every day for two months," she said. "Then started raining twice a day. The clear-cut let water run off the mountain. This whole town's on one slow drown. I'm sick to death of it. My store's got four feet of water in it."

"What kind of store?"

"Frame shop. The wallboard leached the water to the ceiling till it fell in. The light fixtures electrocuted the water snakes. They're still floating on top."

She laughed without changing her eyes or her mouth. It was just a sound coming from her head.

"I cut through here to dodge the flooding," Zules said. "All I had to do was make California and I'd be safe."

"Water runs south."

"I damn sure wish I never."

"I got wishes, too."

"Who don't."

"Not like mine," she said. "I wish I was somebody else. I'm not a good person anymore."

"Maybe you're a little drunk's all."

"I can hold my liquor."

"I ain't saying you can't."

"It's the water," she said. "We don't have anywhere to put it. It won't pile up like snow. It just stays and then it goes bad. Same as me."

"Maybe you should have some coffee."

She stood and leaned against the table.

"I'm not drunk," she said. "I'm sober as a judge."

"That ain't saying much where I'm from."

"Maybe you should go back there."

The woman walked slowly to the door, taking each step in a careful manner, resting her hand on bar stools for support. Zules wished he was the kind of guy who'd follow her home. He ordered another shot. He couldn't quite believe that he'd abandoned a full trailer in Oregon. He felt like a turtle who'd run off and left his shell.

In the morning his head hurt. He turned on the TV and learned that a four-foot wave of water had ripped across the valley. The water had spread over the land like batter in a skillet, covering everything, moving on its own. The phone rang and Zules hoped it was the woman from the night before.

"This is Deputy Terry," a hurried voice said. "We got us a trailer. You'll have to describe yours."

"It's a Peterbilt. Grey and white with Kentucky plates. Mud flaps got chrome bulldogs on them."

"Son of a bitch. We got somebody else's rig."

"Regular yard sale out there, ain't it."

The deputy hung up and Zules went to the lounge, suddenly homesick for Kentucky. The hillsides were so steep it was like living in a maze, but it wasn't a place where you could lose a truck trailer. When Zules was home he stayed with his mother, who was seventy-four. As the youngest child, he was supposed to take care of her, but after a few days he'd be restless, ready for straight roads and flat land. His mother said he was like a cat that hadn't been neutered. He said she had a heart like railroad steel.

The TV in the bar requested volunteers to help sandbag the town, and the bartender offered Zules a lift. They drove through streets of water past floating propane tanks tied to trees. Sandbags made walls around buildings—the fancier the business, the higher the wall.

A dull grey sky covered the sun. Zules waded to a line of people passing sandbags. He found a shovel and someone squatted before him with an open bag and he filled it with sand. The damp air was heavy in his lungs. Shrubs were dead from too much rain. A man carrying a video camera with a number three on it stepped around the pile of sand. Beside him was a young man with makeup on his face who wore a fly-fishing vest and a duck hunting cap. He was talking into a microphone.

When the sand ran out, Zules walked through drizzle to a water cooler on the back of a National Guard truck. Soldiers in camouflage held walkie-talkies and damp cigarettes. The deputy sheriff was with them and Zules asked about his trailer.

"Nothing," the deputy said. He spat between his

teeth, using a technique that Zules remembered practicing as a boy. "You didn't see anybody by that dike last night, did you? No hitchhikers or nothing?"

"It was hard to see," Zules said. "Why?"

"Somebody went up there last night and blew that stinking dike open."

"How come?"

"Give that water somewhere to go. It flooded ten thousand acres of cropland. Whoever it was didn't want that river to bust through down here."

"Hell, that's probably everybody, ain't it."

"You're the only man I know by the dike last night."

Zules laughed until he saw the man's face harden.

"A farmer drowned," the deputy said. "You're the only man I know thinks that funny."

"I wasn't laughing at him," Zules said. "I was laughing at you thinking I'd flood my own rig. Ask your state trooper where I come on him. Here I bust my hind end moving sand for your town and you say I'm flooding it. I don't see you doing any shovel work. Your boots ain't even wet."

"Keep it up, son," the deputy said. "Run that mouth and see where you end up at."

"You can't lock a man up for talking. This is America if you didn't know it."

"It's Oregon and I'm the law."

"Damn good thing crime's low."

The deputy's face turned red. The National Guard glanced at each other, trying to hold back grins. The deputy reached for his handcuffs.

"All right," he said. "Let's go."

"I ain't done a thing," Zules said.

The deputy stepped behind him and slid the cuffs over each wrist, squeezing them hard against the bone. He moved Zules through ankle-deep water to a patrol car.

"Hey!" Zules yelled. "Hey, channel three! Here's some news!"

"Shut the hell up," the deputy said.

The camera man began to trot toward Zules and the deputy. Behind him came the man in the fly-fishing vest, holding the microphone over his head like a pistol. A ring of people stood quietly in the flood-water. Zules saw the woman from the bar. She had her hands on her hips, glaring at the deputy. She looked better in the day, the opposite of most women Zules had met in a tavern.

"Officer," the reporter said. "What exactly—"

"Yes," the woman from the bar said. "Just what in the hell do you think you're doing, Kenneth?"

The deputy began moving Zules to the police car. The backseat was bare metal with no door handle, and Zules slumped low to avoid leaning on his cuffed hands. He hoped the video footage stayed on local stations. He'd hate for his mother to see it.

Half an hour later, Zules was sitting in the county jail's common room, watching a television bolted high on the wall. Below it was a pay phone that didn't work. The other prisoner had the TV remote in his shirt pocket and a toothbrush in his mouth. He introduced himself as Sheetrock James, kin to Jesse. His hands were small, with the shortest fingers Zules had ever seen. The ends were chewed so badly that the nails were tiny spots surrounded by raw skin. His crime was wrecking a dump truck at a landfill.

"Best thing was me getting arrested," he said

around the toothbrush. "I'm staying right here till the flood's over. How high's that water getting to be? You ain't in here on murder, are you?"

Zules shook his head. A soap opera was playing on TV, what his mother called "the stories." His mother never talked about neighbors, but gossiped about TV characters in an intimate way.

"Hey," Zules said to Sheetrock. "Your mama watch TV shows like this?"

"Ain't got one."

"No TV?"

"Mama," Sheetrock said. "I mean I was born from one. Just that she died when I was two. My daddy shot her. She was holding me on the porch, and he shot her twice. They say she set down easy to not let me fall. Daddy, he got twelve years over it. Then he went back to Oklahoma."

Zules regretted that he'd started talking. He'd been in jail before and the best way to get through it was with silence, same as at his mother's house.

"Wake me up when the news comes on," he said.

"Sure thing, man. No problem. You must be one of those people who can take naps. I wish I was. I'm up half the night. It's like I can hear myself talk in my own head."

"Hush, now."

"Yeah, man. Sure. If anyone else comes in, I'll tell them to be quiet."

Zules closed his eyes. When Sheetrock started yelling, Zules knew he'd been asleep. For a few seconds he was disoriented, until the slow realization that he had awakened in a cage. It was a terrible feeling.

"Hey man, it's you!" Sheetrock was pointing at the TV. "You're a goddamn star. Look."

The reporter said that a trucker had been arrested for blowing the dike. There was a final shot of Zules in the police car. Zules had never seen himself on camera and didn't care for his appearance. He looked rough, like someone from the worst hollows at home, a man who belonged in the back of a police car.

"Just think of it," Sheetrock said. "Me celling with a hardcase. I never knew nobody on TV before." He offered Zules the remote. "Here, wish I had more to give."

Zules waved it away and fought down the urge to

pace. He didn't mind getting locked up and he didn't really blame the sheriff. Cops were just guys doing a job. Zules couldn't think of much worse work except maybe driving a truck.

The jailer brought two trays of food into the common room. He gave Zules a hard stare and left. Zules ate the sandwich of baloney on white bread. He gave his cake to Sheetrock.

"Thanks, man," Sheetrock said. "Guess you're watching your weight, huh. What I wouldn't give for a pork chop right now. The water done jumped through this town, man. Worst flooding ever. TV preacher said God did it on account of Portland's porn shops."

The jailer came back with his mouth tight. Sheetrock started eating faster.

"Take your time," the jailer said. "Your cellie here's out. Somebody paid his damn bail."

Zules looked at Sheetrock as if seeing him for the first time. His clothes didn't fit and he needed a haircut. The toothbrush stuck out of his mouth like a handle as he ate.

"Want me to see about you getting out?" Zules said. "Bail can't be all that high on a car wreck."

"Nope. I'm a stayer. That water is bad for my nerves. It won't get in here, either. These cells are on the second floor up. Best place to be just now."

"I could bring you something."

"I got everything I want right here, man. You ought to stay, too. Lot to be said for a man who stays put."

The jailer led Zules to an office where he signed a form to get his wallet, keys, and the gourd. He figured the news had gone national and somebody at home had seen it. He was surprised they'd got him out so fast.

"Who paid my bail?" he said.

"Somebody went through a town lawyer." The jailer opened the main door. "Come back now," he said.

Outside it was dusk and raining again. The water table was above the ground with nowhere to go and Zules felt caught in a crossfire from above and below. He'd heard that there was no new water in the world, that it was all a million years old, evaporating and coming back as rain. He wondered where the hole was that was left by the storms. Maybe the oceans were lower.

A car slowed behind him. The woman from the bar opened the passenger door and he got into the car. She wore a long vinyl poncho. Her bare legs ran into heavy galoshes.

"Are you hungry?" she said.

"Yes, but I don't much feel like eating."

"How was it?"

"Not bad. They got cable in there. They had that at home, half the boys would get locked up just to watch their shows."

"Where's home?"

"Kentucky."

"What part?"

"The part people leave. You from herebouts?"

"Born and bred, except for five years in school at Corvallis. Halfway through I changed my major from science to art. My whole worldview went from the left hemisphere of my brain to the right, just like that."

Zules nodded. He didn't know what she was talking about.

"Sometimes I feel like an English novel translated into Chinese. It's backwards and upside down, and you read it in the opposite direction. Know what I mean?"

He nodded again. People who'd gone to college made him nervous. He always felt as if they looked down on him, were waiting for a chance to make him sound stupid. He'd learned to be quiet around them, and eventually he discovered that his silence made them nervous.

She pulled into a driveway and shut off the engine and got out of the car. Zules followed her. The small house was jammed with boxes stacked on furniture. Everything was off the floor. She pulled a bottle of vodka from a cabinet and poured two shots.

"Mi casa es tu casa," she said.

She swallowed the vodka and filled the glass again. Zules sipped his drink, wondering if what she'd said was from that backward Chinese book.

She opened a door and went down wooden steps and Zules followed. Water was seeping along cracks in the basement walls. An arched stream spouted from the corner like a fountain. Several inches of water ran steadily across the floor toward a hole in the corner. She shoved a stick into the opening. There was a dull click and the sound of a motor.

"Sump pump's got a short," she said.

"Kindly risky in all this wet."

"It's what I'm down to for risks. I have to start a bad habit just to have one to quit."

"I gave up smokes."

"Me, too. Plus pot, the dog track, and demolition derbies. The older I get, the harder it is not to be bored. Travel does it for you, I guess."

"Well, I'm in new places pretty regular."

"Must be nice."

"Don't reckon," he said. "Once you leave a place, you're sort of plowed under for living there again. I don't stay nowhere but the truck mostly."

"I shouldn't have come back here after school. I guess that's what ruined me."

"You don't look all that ruint."

"I figure guys like you have every kind of connection."

"Well, I got cousins all through Ohio."

"That's not what I meant."

Zules nodded, glad that the basement was dark

and she couldn't see his face turning red. She stepped close to him.

"You know why I wear a wedding ring?" she said.

"No."

"To remind me not to sleep with married men."

"I ain't married."

She kissed him and he could taste the vodka. Her poncho squeaked. She went up stone steps to a tornado hatch and pushed it open. Warm air blew into the cellar. Zules climbed the steps to a backyard where lilac bushes grew lush from three months of rain. The storm hid the stars. The sound of thunder spread across the night.

A quick gust jerked the woman's poncho and he could see the pale flash of skin. She took his hand and tugged him to the middle of the yard and kissed him. He smelled the lilacs and the rain. She began to unbuckle his belt. He slid his hands beneath her poncho and was astonished to realize that she was naked. Her skin was wet. The storm pelted them with water. Wind lifted the poncho and she tugged it over her head and it disappeared into the darkness as if yanked by a rope. Very slowly they sank to the ground. The earth was soft. She rolled him on his back.

Rain ran into Zules's mouth and his eyes and his nose. He no longer knew where the water ended and the earth began. The storm crossed overhead, rain flying in all directions, the bellow of thunder within each drop. From a long ways away he could hear someone moaning. The sky was black and the air was warm. The moaning voice became his own. In a quick flash of lightning he saw her above him, her arched body streaming water, her face aimed at the sky, the veins straining in her neck. She resembled someone fighting not to drown.

The storm moved rapidly east, leaving a drizzle that tapered away. High in the night, a speck soon became one of many stars. He felt her breathing become normal. His mind relaxed, moving in various directions at once. He thought of her basement, which reminded him of jail, and he realized that she'd been waiting for him on the street.

"Was it you who bailed me out?" he said.

"You guessed."

"How much it run you?"

"Six."

"I can't pay you back anywhere soon."

"That's not important."

"What'd you do it for?"

She didn't say anything.

"Not for this," he said. "You didn't get me out just to bring me here, did you?"

"No. I'm not that hard up."

"Well, why then?"

"That deputy hasn't slept in three days. The flood's just too big for him. Sort of over his head. You're the first person he saw all summer that he didn't have a history with. He's not really that mean."

"Sounds like you know him pretty good."

"He's my brother."

Zules became tense, aware that the air had turned chilly and he was lying in mud. Kentucky had high ground, woods to hide in, and thousands of creeks to drain the water. When he was home, he felt smothered by hills. Now he was trapped by flood. He'd been safer in jail. A part of him envied Sheetrock for knowing exactly what he wanted. Zules chuckled.

"What?" she said.

"Nothing. Just a guy in jail."

"It should be me."

"You wouldn't like it."

"Maybe not," she said. "But I'm guilty."

"Everyone is of something."

"I mean really guilty."

"You don't have to tell me nothing."

"It was me who blew that dike."

She began to cry and he held her.

"I thought it would take the pressure off down here," she said. "You know, save the town from getting flooded out. I wanted to help people, but that man died. It's the same as if I killed him."

Zules gave the woman a long, tight hug and gently lifted her off him. She was shivering. Her wet hair made her head look small. He led her into the house and poured vodka, which seemed to revive her. Water pooled on the floor where they stood. Zules closed his pants and buckled his belt, feeling awkward since she was naked. A mosquito hummed past his ear. He wanted to say something but didn't know what. She spoke instead.

"You just go around living however you want. Must be nice to be that free."

"Except for going to jail."

"That's all this town is. One big jail of water."

Zules slid his hand in his pocket and offered her the little gourd. The seeds rattled. She held it in cupped hands, dripping water.

"For luck," he said.

"I hurt all over."

"I know."

"There's no need to stay," she said, "or go."

He wondered what she wanted but didn't know how to find out. He moved to the door, still looking at her. Mud ran up her legs past her knees, reminding him of old-fashioned stockings. She was holding the gourd. As he left he realized how lovely her shoulders were.

Zules began walking, unsure of direction and not really caring. The night sky had temporarily cleared to a black sheen filled with stars. He could feel the water in his boots, the weight of mud on his back. He shut down his mind and walked, glad for the necessity of motion. From everywhere came the steady sound of dripping water.

A police car slowed in a crossroads and stopped beside him. The deputy was driving. He wasn't wearing his uniform, and Zules felt as if a hellhound had finally found his trail. As the water rose, he was sinking. He was going to be killed and lost in the flood and he didn't really care. He was tired. For his mother's sake, he hoped that someone would find his body. It occurred to him that dying on a cold wet night was no worse than a fine autumn day.

"How's she doing?" the deputy said.

"My mother? They'll knock her in the head on Judgment Day."

"You know who I mean," the deputy said. "Is she all right?"

"Not exactly."

"Get in."

"I'm pretty bad muddy."

"Doesn't matter. It's a county car."

"I don't really need a lift."

"Just get in the stinking car. I'll run you by your motel."

Zules slid in the front seat and the deputy made a U-turn. He drove past blinking yellow lights on sawhorses that blocked flooded streets. All the houses were dark. People sat on the porches holding flashlights and rifles.

The deputy stopped at the motel. A maple by the door had been hit by lightning and the lot was covered with wood chips and twigs. Zules could smell the fresh scent of the tree's inner meat. The burn mark ran to the ground.

"Charges are dropped," the deputy said.

"That state trooper clear me?"

"No. We got a witness. An old man saw a car leaving the scene. He can put the driver in it, too."

The deputy sighed. He shifted his body toward Zules. His voice was low and sad, defeated.

"I know who did it."

"Anyone else know?" Zules said.

"Not unless you do."

"What about the witness?"

"He's an old river rat," the deputy said. "Long as he don't get busted for running trotlines, he won't say nothing."

"And if he did, nobody'd believe him."

"About like you."

"In that case," Zules said, "I best be leaving."

A shower came over the car, the drops rapid as if a squirrel ran along the roof. The rain moved down the street. The motel's neon sign abruptly went out.

Lightning flashed on the horizon and Zules realized that he'd been hearing the dull rumble of thunder for a long time. It was coming from everywhere, like the rain.

He opened the car door but the deputy's voice stopped him. "I don't know what to do. I thought I did but I'm not sure anymore. You ever get that way?"

"That's why I left home."

"I've never lived anywhere but this place."

"How come you to be a cop?"

"Just like to see things run smooth, I guess. I know everybody here, who their folks are and their kids. Every little thing they do. I know who steals and who looks in windows and who sleeps with who. I'm tired of it, too. But the knowing keeps me here."

"Same thing drove me off my home hill."

The deputy grinned, a thin expression that was gone fast. "Real reason is, ten years ago I couldn't afford a car. I let the county give me one."

"That's why I took my first driving job."

"But you can move on."

"I'd rather be a stayer."

Zules walked to his truck and climbed into the cab. He let the engine warm up, feeling its power vibrate through his body, relaxing him. He felt safe. It was the highest above ground he'd been since leaving jail. Sheetrock was right about the safety of the cell. Zules decided to give him a call in a few days, same as he would his mother.

Zules opened his map and stared at the red and blue highway lines until they blurred like veins under skin. He was pretty close to the edge of the country, with nowhere to go. He sat in the truck for a long time, looking into the darkness. The wet land was flat as tin. He decided to head home for good. He was thirty-one, with no ex-wife and a little money. There'd be someone to marry him. He could get his own place then. He'd sell the truck and apply for work, maybe as a cop. He thought he'd make a good one.

Rain fell in waves and his headlights were dull against the fog. He put the truck in gear and headed home, moving into second and third carefully. It was dangerous to drive fast without a trailer behind him. He needed a heavy load to keep him stable.

Barred Owl

Seven years ago I got divorced and left Kentucky, heading west. I made the Mississippi River in one day, and it just floored me how big it was. I watched the water until sundown. It didn't seem like a river, but a giant brown muscle instead. Two days later, my car threw a rod and I settled in Greeley, Colorado. Nobody in my family has lived this far off our home hill.

I took a job painting dorm rooms at the college here in town. The pay wasn't the best, but I could go to work hungover and nobody bugged me. I liked the quiet of working alone. I went into a room and

made it a different color. The walls and the ceiling
hadn't gone anywhere, but it was a new place. Only
the view from the window stayed the same. What I
did was never look out.

Every day after work I stopped by the Pig's Eye,
a bar with cheap draft, a pool table, and a jukebox. It
was the kind of place to get drunk in safely, because
the law watched student bars downtown. The
biggest jerk in the joint was the bartender. He liked
to throw people out. You could smoke reefer in the
Pig, gamble and fight, but if you drank too much,
you were barred. That always struck me odd—like
throwing someone out of a hospital for being sick.

Since my social life was tied to the Pig, I was surprised when a man came to the house one Saturday
afternoon. That it was Tarvis surprised me even
more. He's from eastern Kentucky, and people often mentioned him, but we'd never met. His hair
was short and his beard was long. I invited him in.

"Thank ye, no," he said.

I understood that he knew I was just being polite,
that he wouldn't enter my house until my welcome
was genuine. I stepped outside, deliberately leaving
the door open. What happened next was a ritual the

likes of which I'd practically forgotten, but once it began, felt like going home with an old girlfriend you happened to meet in a bar.

We looked each other in the eyes for a spell.

Tarvis nodded slightly.

I nodded slightly.

He opened a pouch of Red Man and offered a chew.

I declined and began the slow process of lighting a cigarette while he dug a wad of tobacco from the pouch.

I flicked the match away, and we watched it land.

He worked his chew and spat, and we watched it hit in the grass. Our hands were free. We'd shown that our guard was down enough to watch something besides each other.

"Nice house," he said.

"I rent."

"Weather ain't too awful bad this spring."

"Always use rain."

"Keep dogs?" he said.

"Used to."

"Fish?"

"Every chance I get."

He glanced at me and quickly away. It was my turn now. If you don't hear an accent you lose it, and just being around him made me talk like home.

"Working hard?" I said.

"Loafing."

"Get home much?"

"Weddings and funerals."

"I got it down to funerals myself," I said.

"Only place I feel at home anymore is the grave-yard."

He spat again, and I stubbed out my cigarette. A half moon had been hanging in the sky since late afternoon as if waiting for its chance to move.

"Hunt?" he asked.

I spat then, a tiny white dab near his darker pool, mine like a star, his an eclipse. I hadn't hunted since moving here. Hunters in the West used four-wheel-drive go-carts with a gunrack on the front and a cargo bin behind. They lived in canvas wall-tents that had woodstoves and cots. I'd seen them coming and going like small armies in the mountains. People at home hunted alone on foot. Tarvis looked every inch a hunter and I decided not to get into it with him.

"Not like I did," I said.

He nodded and looked at me straight on, which meant the reason for his visit was near.

"Skin them out yourself?" he said.

I nodded.

"Come by my place tomorrow, then."

He gave me directions and drove away, his arm hanging out the window. I figured he needed help dressing out a deer. I'm not big on poaching but with the deer already dead, refusing to help meant wasting the meat.

I headed for the bar, hoping to meet a woman. The problem with dating in a college town is that the young women are too young, and the older ones usually have kids. I've dated single mothers but it's hard to know if you like the woman or the whole package. A ready-made home can look awful good. Women with kids tell me it's just as tricky for them. Men figure they're either hunting a full-time daddy or some overnight action, with nothing in between.

This night was the usual Pig crowd, my friends of seven years. I drank straight shots and at last call ordered a couple of doubles. I'd started out drinking to feel good but by the end I was drinking not to feel anything. During the drive home I had to look away from the road to prevent the center stripe from splitting. I fixed that by straddling it. In the morning I woke fully dressed on my couch.

Four cigarettes and a cup of coffee later I felt alive enough to visit Tarvis. He lived below town on a dirt road beside the South Platte River. I veered around a dead raccoon with a tire trench cut through its guts. There were a couple of trailers and a few small houses. Some had outdoor toilets. At Tarvis's house I realized why the area seemed both strangely foreign and familiar. It was a little version of eastern Kentucky, complete with woodpiles, cardboard windows, and a lousy road. The only thing missing was hills.

I'd woke up still drunk and now that I was getting sober, the hangover was coming on. I wished I'd brought some beer. I got nervous that Tarvis had killed his deer in a hard place and needed help dragging it out of the brush. I didn't think I could take it. What I needed was to lie down for a while.

Tarvis came around the house from the rear.

"Hidy," he said. "Ain't too awful late, are ye?"

"Is it on the property?"

He led me behind the house to a line of cottonwoods overlooking the river's floodplain. A large bag lay on a work table. Tarvis reached inside and very gently, as if handling eggs, withdrew a bird. The feathers on its chest made a pattern of brown and white—a barred owl. Its wings spanned four feet. The head feathers formed a widow's peak between the giant eyes. It had a curved yellow beak and inch-long talons. Tarvis caressed its chest.

"Beaut, ain't it?" he said. "Not a mark to her."

"You kill it?"

"No. Found it on the interstate up by Fort Morgan. It hit a truck or something. Neck's broke."

The sun had risen above the trees, streaming heat and light against my face. Owls were protected by the government. Owning a single feather was illegal, let alone the whole bird.

"I want this pelt," Tarvis said.

"Never done a bird."

"You've skinned animals out. Can't be that big a difference."

"Why don't you do it yourself then?"

Tarvis backstepped as an expression close to guilt passed across his face.

"I never skinned nothing," he said. "Nobody

taught me on account of I never pulled the trigger. I was raised to it, but I just wasn't able."

I looked away to protect his dignity. His words charged me with a responsibility I couldn't deny, the responsibility of Tarvis's shame. Leaving would betray a confidence that had taken a fair share of guts to tell.

I felt dizzy, but I rolled my sleeves up and began with the right leg. Surrounding the claws were feathers so dense and fine that they reminded me of fur. To prevent tearing the papery skin, I massaged it off the meat. Tarvis stood beside me. I held the owl's body and slowed turned it, working the skin free. My arms cooled from the breeze, and I could smell the liquor in my sweat. The hangover was beginning to lift. I snipped the cartilage and tendon surrounding the large wing bone, and carefully exposed the pink muscle. Feathers scraped the plywood like a broom. The owl was giving itself to me, giving its feathered pelt and its greatest gift, that which separated it from us—the wings. In return I'd give it a proper burial.

There is an intensity to skinning, a sense of immediacy. Once you start, you must continue. Many people work fast to get it over with, but I like to take it slow. I hadn't felt this way in a long time and hadn't known I'd missed it.

I eased the skin over the back of the skull. Its right side was caved in pretty bad. The pelt was inside out, connected to the body at the beak, as if the owl was kissing the shadow of its mate. I passed it to Tarvis. He held the slippery skull in one hand and gently tugged the skin free of the carcass.

"Get a shovel," I said.

Tarvis circled the house for a spade and dug a hole beneath a cottonwood. I examined the bird. Both legs, the skull, each wing, its neck and ribs—all were broken. It's head hung from several shattered vertebrae. I'd never seen a creature so clean on the outside and so tore up on the inside. It had died pretty hard.

I built a twig platform and placed the remains in the grave. Tarvis began to spade the dirt in. He tamped it down, mumbling to himself. I reversed the pelt so the feathers were facing out. The body cavity flattened to an empty skin, a pouch with wings that would never fly.

Hand-shaking is not customary among men in eastern Kentucky. We stood apart from one another and nodded, arms dangling, boots scuffing the dirt, as if our limbs were useless without work.

"Got any whiskey?" I said.

"Way I drank gave it a bad name. Quit when I left Kentucky."

"That's when I took it up. What makes you want that owl so bad?"

"It's pure built to hunt. Got three ear holes and it flies silent. It can open and close each pupil separate from the other one. They ain't a better hunter."

"Well," I said. "Reckon you know your owls."

I drove to the bar for a few shots and thought about eating, but didn't want to ruin a ten-dollar drunk with a five-dollar meal. I didn't meet a woman and didn't care. When the bar closed, a bunch of us bought six-packs and went to my house. I laid drunk through most of the week, thinking about Tarvis in the blurred space between hangover and the day's first drink. Though I'd shown him how to skin, I had the feeling he was guiding me into something I'd tried to leave behind.

A few weeks later I met a teacher who was considering a move to Kentucky because it was a place

that could use her help. We spent a few nights together. I felt like a test for her, a way of gauging Kentucky's need. I guess I flunked because she moved to
South Dakota for a job on the Sioux Reservation.

On Memorial Day I took a six-pack of dog hair to
Tarvis's house, parked behind his truck, and opened
a beer. At first I wanted to gag, but there's no better
buzz than a drink on an empty stomach. I drank half
and held it down. The heat spread through my body,
activating last night's bourbon. I finished the beer
and opened another.

Tarvis came out of the house, blinking against
the sun. We went to the riverbank and sat in metal
chairs. A great blue heron flew north, its neck curled
like a snake ready to strike. The air was quiet. We
could have been by the Blue Lick River back home.
It felt right to sit with someone of the hills, even if
we didn't have a lot to say.

I asked to see the owl and Tarvis reluctantly led
me to the door. His eyes were shiny as new dimes.
"Ain't nobody been inside in eight years."

The cabin was one room with a sink, range, toilet, and mattress. A woodstove stained from tobacco

spit stood in the middle. The only furniture was a tattered couch. Shelves lined every wall, filled with things he'd found in the woods.

A dozen owl pellets lay beside a jumble of antlers. A variety of bird wings were pinned to the wall. One shelf held sun-bleached bones and another contained thirty or forty jaw bones. Skulls were jammed in—raccoon, fox, deer, a dozen groundhog. Hundreds of feathers poked into wall cracks and knotholes. There were so many feathers that I had the sense of being within the owl pelt turned inside out.

Tarvis pulled a board from the highest shelf. The owl lay on its back, wings stretched full to either side. The claws hung from strips of downy hide. Tarvis had smoothed the feathers into their proper pattern.

"You did a good job," I said.

"Had some help."

"Ever find Indian stuff?"

"All this came from hunting arrowheads," he said. "But I never found one. Maybe I don't know how to look."

"Maybe this is what finds you."

He handed me a stick from one of the shelves. It was eighteen inches long, sanded smooth and feathered at one end. He reached under the couch for a handmade bow.

"That's osage orangewood," he said. "Same as the Indians used. I made them both. Soon's I find me a point I'll be setting pretty."

"You going to hunt with it?"

"No." He looked away. "I don't even kill mosquitoes. What I do is let the spiders go crazy in here. They keep the bugs down and snakes stop the mice. Hawks eat the snakes. Fox kills the duck. An owl hunts everything, but nothing hunts the owl. It's like man."

He put the owl on a shelf and opened the door. We went outside. The staccato of a woodpecker came across the river, each peck distinct as a bell.

"How come you don't hunt?" I said.

He looked at me, then away, and back to me. His eyes were smoky.

"I don't know," he said. "Hear that woodpecker? Take and cut its beak off and it'll pound its face against a tree until it dies. Not hunting does me the same way. But I still can't do it."

The river shimmered in the wind, sunlight catching each tiny cresting wave. A breeze carried the scent of clover and mud. I slipped away to my car.

Work hit a slow spell. I was in a dorm I'd painted twice before and could do it blindfolded. The rooms repeated themselves, each one a mirror image of the last. I went in and out of the same room over and over. Sometimes I didn't know where I was, and leaving didn't help because the hallway was filled with identical doors.

The next time I visited Tarvis, I drank the neck and shoulders out of a fifth while he talked. He was from a family of twelve. His last name was Eldridge. He grew up on Eldridge Ridge, overlooking Eldridge Creek in Eldridge County. His people numbered so many that they got identified by hair color and their mother's maiden name. Nobody called him Tarvis. He was Ida Cumbow's fourth boy, a black-headed Eldridge. That's what finally made him leave. No one knew who he was.

Tarvis and I sat till the air was greyed by dusk. Night covered us over. We were like a pair of seashells a long way from the beach. If you held one of us to your ear, you'd hear Kentucky in the distance, but listening to both would put you flat in the woods.

An owl called from the river.

"There's your owl," I said.

"No, that's a great horned. A barred owl getting this far west ain't right."

"Maybe that's why it died."

Tarvis looked at me for a spell, his eyes gleaming in the darkness. He never spoke and I left for the Pig. The ease of Tarvis's company just drove in the fact that I didn't belong out here. Maybe that's why I drank so much that night. I woke up the next day filled with dread, craving water, and with no memory of what had happened at the bar. I used to think not remembering meant I'd had a great time. Now I know it for a bad sign, but a drink can cut that fear like a scythe.

I went back to see Tarvis at the height of summer. The river moved so slowly it seemed to be still, a flat pane of reflected light. Mosquitoes began to circle my head. Tarvis opened his door, squinting against the sun. He'd lost weight. His hands were crusted with dirt and he reminded me of the old men at home, weary from slant-farming hillsides that never yielded enough.

We nodded to each other, began the ritual of tobacco. His voice sounded rusty and cracked. He moved his lips before each word, forming the word itself.

"Found one," he said.

I knew immediately what he meant.

"Where?"

"Creek. Four mile downriver. Half mile in."

"Flint?"

His head moved in a slow shake.

"Chert," he said. "No flint in America."

"You make the arrow?"

He shivered. Mosquitoes rose from his body and we looked at each other a long time. He never blinked. I smacked a mosquito against my neck. He compressed his lips and went back inside, softly closing the door.

I spent the rest of the summer drinking and didn't think about Tarvis anymore. For a while I dated a woman, if you can call it that. We drank till the bar closed, then went to her house and tried not to pass out in the middle of everything. It eventually went to hell between us. Everybody said it would. She liked to laugh, though, and nothing else really mattered.

The day we split up, I got drunk at the Pig. Someone was in the men's room, and I went in the women's. It was commonly done. The uncommon part was falling through the window. The bartender didn't ask what happened or if I was hurt, just barred me on the spot. He thought I threw a garbage can through the window. He said that nothing human had broken it, and I wondered what he thought I was.

I took my drinking down the street, but it wasn't the same. I was homesick for the Pig.

A few months later a policeman arrived at my house and I got scared that I'd hit someone with my car. I was always finding fresh dents and scraped paint in the morning. The cop was neckless and blond, officially polite. He asked if I knew Tarvis Eldridge and I nodded. He asked if the deceased had displayed any behavior out of the ordinary and I told him no, wanting to side with Tarvis even dead.

"A will left his house to you," the cop said.

"Maybe he wasn't right when he wrote it."

"We don't think he was," the cop said. "But the house is yours."

He stood to leave, and I asked how Tarvis had died. In a slow, embarrassed fashion, he told me part of it. I went to the county coroner who filled in the gaps. It was his most unusual case, and he talked about it like a man who'd pulled in a ten-inch trout on a dime-store rod.

Tarvis had fastened one end of the bow to an iron plate and screwed the plate to the floor. Guy wires held the bow upright. He fitted an arrow with a chert point into the bow, drew it tight, and braced it. A strip of rawhide ran across the floor to the couch where they found him. All he had to do was pull the leather cord to release the arrow.

His body had been sent home for burial. As much as he'd tried to get out, the hills had claimed him.

I drove to Tarvis's house and gathered his personal stuff—a toothbrush and comb, his tobacco pouch, knife, and hat. I dug a hole beside the owl's grave and dropped it all in. It seemed fitting that he'd have two graves, one here and another in Kentucky. I filled the hole and smoothed the earth and didn't know what to say. Everything I came up with sounded stupid. It was such a small place in the ground. I wasn't burying him, I was covering over how I felt.

I left for town. My neighborhood was neat and clean, like dorm walls after a fresh coat. From the outside, my house looked like all the rest. The refrigerator held lunchmeat, eggs, and milk. The toilet ran unless you jiggled the handle. I didn't even go in. I bought a pint for later and drove to the Pig, forgetting that I'd been barred. I sat in the car outside. The windows of the tavern were brightly lit and I knew everyone in there. I'd not been to the Pig for three months and none of my friends had called me, not a one.

I drove back to Tarvis's road, pulled over, and cut the engine. I hadn't known how tore up the inside of the owl was, and I couldn't tell about Tarvis either. Both of them should have stayed in the woods. It made me wonder if I should have. I opened the whiskey. The smell was quick and strong, and I threw the full bottle out the car window. I don't know why. As soon as I did, I regretted it. The bottle didn't break and I heard the bourbon emptying into the ditch. I knew it wouldn't all run out.

I went down the road and parked in the shadow of Tarvis's house. The river was dark and flat. Long-eared owls were calling to each other, answering and calling. There was one female calling and three males hollering back, which reminded me of the Pig. Maybe Tarvis would still be living if he'd let himself take a drink to get through the hard parts. He'd gotten himself home, though, while I was still stuck out here in the world. I suddenly thought of something that drained me like a shell. I sat in the dark listening to the owls but there was no way for me to get around it. I missed Kentucky more than the Pig.

Target Practice

Ray set a log on the chopping block and swung the heavy maul. The seasoned ash split easily. He switched to the hatchet and cut thin strips of kindling that curved around knots and fell to the ground. The effort loosened a tension that had become habit since his return to the hills. He'd left Kentucky several years ago and now he wished he'd stayed on the assembly line at the Chrysler plant in Detroit.

The house didn't have a bathroom and his woodstove leaked smoke indoors. The clay dirt wouldn't hold a garden. His wife had left him and Ray was too embarrassed to tell anyone.

A truck ground into a lower gear and Ray recognized the sound of the trashman's pickup. Once a month everyone on the hill left money in a jar on top of their garbage cans. Ray's father, Franklin, was the only person who made the trashman walk to his house and ask him for the money.

Three years back, Franklin quit work and began staying at home. His wife was dead. A neighbor brought him groceries. Twice a day he went outside to chop wood, though he had a gas furnace. Split cordwood was stacked high around his house. He hadn't been off the hill in three years. As the neighbors said, Franklin had a funny turn to him.

The trash truck sprayed gravel climbing the steep bank of Ray's driveway. Ray dropped the hatchet and walked to the pickup.

"Chopping wood?" the trashman said.

"Can't get enough."

"Hear ol' Franklin's got a regular sawmill full."

"Yeah," Ray said. "I'm planning to raid him the first dark night."

The trashman laughed and showed Ray a semi-automatic rifle. It was old and plain.

"You'll need this," he said. "Swapped a dog for a VCR and got this to boot. Take twenty for it."

Ray shook his head.

"Here," the trashman said, "see how it shoots."

Ray took the rifle. He opened the breech and saw a bullet. He was truly home—a man he barely knew had passed him a loaded weapon.

The trashman pointed at the slope behind the house.

"Hit that stump up yonder," he said.

Ray peered down the barrel. He put the stump in the sight and squeezed the trigger. The rifle made a sharp crack and in the same second a bullet smacked the poplar stump. Birds lifted from the brush and sound stopped. Ray suddenly wanted the gun.

"Don't know if I got twenty," Ray said.

"Clean it up and it's a forty-dollar gun."

"See that milkweed pod?"

The trashman nodded, a barely perceptible move of his head. Ray aimed and deliberately missed.

"Sights ain't right," he said. "Give you ten."

The trashman spat in the dirt. He took the gun, climbed in his truck, and started the engine. He jerked his chin to Ray.

"Take fifteen," the trashman said.

"Throw in some shells?"

The trashman nodded and Ray went in the house for money. The trashman tucked the cash in his shirt pocket without counting it. He flipped his cigarette in the yard.

"Franklin run me off for that once," the trashman said.

"What?"

"Throwing a butt in his yard."

"Don't doubt it," Ray said. He aimed the rifle up the hillside. "He's run me off a few times, too."

The trashman thought that was funny.

"Run you off," he said. "Your own daddy."

Ray let his face turn blank and cold, staring at the man until he backed the truck down the drive and out the ridge. Ray fired several times at the stump, adjusting the sight to correct the slight pull to the left. He aimed at the milkweed pod. It exploded in a burst of feathery white that drifted on the breeze.

136

In Detroit he went to a bar after work where other Kentuckians drank. Ray had met his wife there. She was from Hazel Park, a neighborhood so full of Appalachians it was called Hazel-tucky. Her parents had headed north for work in the sixties. Having grown up with stories of the hills, she'd been enthusiastic about her return until winter in the cold house. They slept on a couchbed with an electric blanket. There was a separate control for each side of the blanket and Ray kept the heat low on her side, hoping she'd roll his way in the night. Instead, she wore long johns. At the first sign of spring, she called a cousin who came for her. Ray didn't blame her. He only wished she'd talked to him first.

He went inside and called his father's house. After several rings, his father grunted into the phone.

"I just bought a rifle," Ray said. "A repeater. Want to come and try it?"

"I don't know," his father said.

After a long silence, Ray said good-bye and kicked the phone across the floor. He figured his father would view the call as weakness. Franklin had not visited Ray since he'd been back, although they lived on the same hill, at opposite ridges.

Ray looked through the window at tufts of grass struggling in the clay dirt. It was his dirt and his grass and his house. The dream of all Kentuckians in Detroit was to come home for good. Now that he was back, he realized that people here wanted to be left alone. There was more community at the Chrysler plant than on his home hill.

Ten minutes after the phone call, Ray was surprised to see his father climb the gravel driveway and stop at the boundary ditch. The sun pushed Franklin's shadow across the yard. He wore a hat, long coat, and boots. He was carrying a rifle. Ray shook his head. He should have figured his father would visit if he could come armed.

Ray slipped ten rounds into the ammo slot and tipped the rifle, hearing the bullets slide down the track. He chambered a final slug and clicked the dull red button to lock the trigger. He went outside. Franklin stared at him from the property's edge, and Ray realized that he was waiting for a greeting. This was Ray's land. It was on him to speak first.

A dog began barking along the ridge. Another

answered from down the hill. Ray recognized each voice, knew their owners. A crow called from the tree line. Franklin and Ray watched each other as the hounds continued to bark.

"Dogs," Ray said.

"Ought to be shot."

"There's a flat spot on top of the hill," Ray said. "It's a good place for us."

He tipped his head to an old logging trail thick with horseweed, and waited for his father. Franklin went around the woodpile. He picked up the hatchet.

"Shouldn't ought to leave this laying around," he said. "Somebody might get hurt."

He held the hatchet in front of his face as if aiming at Ray. In a swift motion, Franklin sank the blade into a log and stepped past his son. He began to climb the hill, grunting with effort.

Ray left the path for a shortcut. He crossed the ditch and used saplings to pull himself up the slope. Sawbriars raked his clothes, bit into his arms and legs. He was snared and his father was already nearing the top. It would take time to work himself free, or he could plunge forward and hope none stabbed too deep. Ray swept his arm at an angle against the thorns. A thick briar whipped the air and tore his jaw. Squatting, he wiggled like a pup beneath the interlaced overhang and crawled out.

His father leaned on a knee, his breath coming hard. Behind him a nuthatch walked headfirst down a pine trunk. Woodsmoke drifted the air. The dogs were quiet.

"Looks like you got waylaid," Franklin said.

Ray touched the welt and wiped blood on his pants.

"Just briars is all."

Ray walked to the end of the clearing where a caved-in pony pen sat among walnut trees. He placed four nuts on a rotted board, wondering if his father's rifle was loaded. The wind moved sassafras smell along the ridge. A gust rippled Franklin's overcoat and he pushed it awkwardly, reminding Ray of a woman holding down a skirt. He could not recall ever seeing his father anywhere but in his own house or yard. Now, against the barren hillside, Franklin looked vulnerable.

"Headaches staying gone?" Ray said.

"Yes. How's your wife?"

"All right, I guess."

"Not too dirty?"

Ray frowned. His father had always been extremely polite about his daughter-in-law. When Ray brought her to visit, he'd picked lint from her clothes and complimented her hair.

"She needing a shower?" Franklin said.

"Couple more weeks and the bathroom'll be done. Everything takes longer than I think."

"Tell her to come over and get cleaned up."

Ray waited for the invitation to include him, but his father was checking his rifle, and Ray understood that he wasn't really welcome. The house he'd grown up in was no longer home. The whole hill had changed. Town water meant anybody could shove a trailer out a ridge. It was the same as a city, but Detroit was more honest. It didn't pretend to be anything other than what it was—a place where a man could get shot over nothing.

Ray placed an open box of ammunition on a stump. Franklin tugged the bolt and slipped a bullet from his pocket into the breech. A thread clung to the exposed lead.

"Use mine," Ray said. "Copper casing'll keep your barrel from nastying itself up."

"Stayed gone five years and still yet talking like a hillbilly."

"Beats a redneck."

"What's wrong with that? A man who works the land gets sunburnt. My dad's neck was red his whole life."

Franklin looked across the hollow at the pink dogwood dotting the early spring woods. A red-tailed hawk soared beyond a far ridge.

"You and my dad," Franklin said. "You two would've killed each other. See that hawk. He could shoot those out of the air with an army pistol."

"Hard shot."

"He could throw a hatchet like a tomahawk. Make it stick right where he wanted. Said he learned it off his granddaddy, who'd fought that way."

"Pretty tough."

"No, he was what they call a late homosexual. He never liked me much."

Ray followed the hawk's flight above the hill. He didn't believe his father. Franklin's dad had died young, and it occurred to Ray that since Franklin had never been an adult son, maybe he didn't know how to deal with his own.

"What makes you say that about him?" Ray said.

"Right before he died," Franklin said, "he started in wearing flowerdy shirts and going to town at night. Somebody sent roses to the funeral home. There wasn't no card."

"Maybe he had a girlfriend."

"I wouldn't know," Franklin said. "I ain't nothing but the middleman."

"You're more than that."

"If you'd stayed gone, I wouldn't have to be anybody."

Franklin brought the rifle to his shoulder and fired. The sudden noise echoed between the hills and faded down the hollow. Pieces of shattered walnut flew into the brush. He ejected the shell, slipped a fresh bullet in, and shot the second nut.

"Your shot," he said.

Ray nodded, surprised by Franklin's accuracy and the ease with which he handled the gun. The streaked barrel needed blueing, and the burnished walnut stock would be hard to find these days.

Franklin kept it behind a door, wrapped in plastic, with a glove covering the barrel's end. Ray had assumed it was a relic, not a tool Franklin could still use.

Ray centered the wedge in the near sight's notch. He relaxed his shoulders, took a deep breath, and let it out slowly. At the breath's end, he tightened his finger on the trigger. The walnut vanished in a shower of shell. The automatic action ejected the spent cartridge and forced another bullet into the chamber. Ray aimed with care. The barrel swayed and he moved it too far, then overcompensated the other way. His hands were sweaty. He lowered the rifle and blinked into the woods, focusing on the buds of a crab apple tree. A breeze carried its scent his way. Ray raised the rifle, aimed, and shot. Nutshell scattered in the bushes.

He went across the clearing and placed more nuts on the board. As he walked back to his father, Franklin upended the rifle and slipped the barrel in his mouth. He held it steady, looking down the sights in reverse. He hunched his shoulders and bowed his back to accommodate the weapon's length.

Ray knew he couldn't get to him in time. If he made a grab for the rifle, he'd knock his father's teeth out, and Franklin would get mad about that. Ray was struck by a sudden, terrible thought—a shotgun was better for the job.

Franklin inhaled through his nose. He closed his eyes and slowly let his breath go into the gun. His cheeks sank as he blew. He took another breath and did it again. He lowered the rifle and offered it to Ray.

"Barrel's clean now," Franklin said.

Ray crossed the ground to him. As they switched rifles, there was a brief moment when Ray held each gun. He wanted to run down the hill and throw them in the creek. Instead, he released the rifle, unable to resist his father's pull.

"Never shot an automatic before," Franklin said.

He sighted on the first walnut and fired rapidly eight times. Each shot made a quick noise that echoed along the ridge in one long sound until the trigger clicked against the empty chamber. Franklin's face was flushed. He was smiling.

"Always wanted to do that," he said.

Ray aimed his father's heavier gun. The walnut

faded into the mud and seemed to move. He lowered the rifle and shut his eyes, still seeing the gun in his father's mouth. Ray wondered if Franklin had done it just to rattle his aim. When Ray opened his eyes, his father was waiting and Ray shot too fast. The walnut didn't stir.

"I never miss with that," Franklin said. "It was my dad's gun and his dad's before that."

"With any luck," Ray said, "all my children will be girls."

"I wasn't that lucky."

"Neither was your dad."

"No," Franklin said. "Our family's full of hardluck fathers. You know how mine died?"

"Stroke, you always said."

"No. He ate his gun."

His voice was casual, as if they were discussing weather. Every time Franklin talked about his dad, he told a different story. Ray had stopped trying to figure out the truth.

They traded rifles and reloaded. Ray decided to tell him that his wife was gone. They were in similar shape—the last men in their family, living alone on the hill.

"I'm glad you came over," Ray said. "Why do you stay away from me?"

"Because you act like my dad."

"I ain't him."

"You can hurt me just as bad."

"I won't," Ray said.

"You don't know that."

Franklin stared at his son. Ray knew that his father would never look away, that if Ray didn't break the stare, they'd stay there until dark. Ray grinned and turned his body. He didn't stop looking at his father, but slowly pivoted until he was out of sight.

Franklin began walking downhill, his coat flaring behind his stiff back. Ray knew he was very angry. He followed him off the ridge, wondering why things between them had to go bad so fast. When Ray went north, Franklin had criticized him for leaving Kentucky, and Ray thought that buying property and coming home married would make his father like him. Instead, Franklin told him it was stupid to throw away a good job in Detroit.

Mist blurred the ragged seam where the treeline met the sky. This was the highest spot on the hill. It belonged to Ray. He thought he should be proud. Instead, he missed the Chrysler plant. It was dangerous and dirty, but Ray always knew where he stood with people. He could get his old job back. The guys on the line would be glad to see him.

Franklin was standing behind the woodpile at the bottom of the hill. Ray decided to tell him that his wife had left, and that he was leaving, too. When he came within sound range, Franklin spun very fast, the barrel of his rifle pointing at his son. Ray fired twice. The first bullet went wide but the second one made a hole in the part of his father's coat that covered his chest.

Ray felt hot but his skin was cold.

Franklin stepped forward. There was an expression of respect on his face, almost as if he approved of his son. His legs buckled and he fell to his knees. He braced his arms on the chopping block. His eyes were clear as glass.

"My daddy made me kneel on rocks," he said.

He slowly slumped over the chopping block. His hat fell off. The top of his head held a bald spot that was a perfect circle of cleared skin, bright pink. Ray realized that he'd never seen it from above. His own hair was thinning in the same place, following the same pattern. Ray remembered a man with a knife who had tried to rob him outside a bar in Detroit. He'd fought the guy and kept his wallet, and everyone at work told him how stupid it was. Ray had agreed, but he'd reacted without thinking, the same as now.

His father looked as though he was resting, like a child who'd fallen asleep with his head on a table. His shoulders were rising and falling as he breathed. Ray didn't think there was enough blood to have hit an artery. It wasn't so bad.

The sound of an engine carried along the ridge, getting louder as the trash truck's tires spun a rut in the driveway. The trashman leaned out the window. The woodpile blocked his view of Franklin.

"Figured that racket was you," he said.

Ray nodded. The trashman rubbed his jaw and sucked his lower lip between his teeth. His voice was casual.

"If you want, there's other stuff I can get. Shotguns. Pistols and such. They might run you more

than that rifle. How about a belt buckle with a der-
ringer that clips on and off it? Never know when
you need a belly gun."

Ray considered asking the trashman to help him
with Franklin, but decided against it. Assistance
from outside the family was the kind of thing that
his father would resent. He might hold it against
Ray later.

The truck backed down the driveway and Ray
hoped the trashman didn't think his silence was
rude. He went in the house for towels to wrap his
father's wound. It was high on his chest, a clean
hole. The bleeding had already begun to slow.

Ray drove his car around the woodpile, got out,
and studied the situation. It would be easier with a
four-door. He could borrow one from his neighbor
but he didn't want to leave his father that long.

He held Franklin under the armpits and gently
moved him into the car. Twice he had to go around,
climb in the driver's side, and tug on him. As he circled the car, Ray realized that he'd never touched
his father before. He couldn't remember a hug from
him or even a squeeze of his shoulder.

He finally got him wedged inside. Blood was

coming from under the towels. It had gotten on Ray's hands and he wiped them on his pants. He sat in the driver's seat and rested. Franklin's face was relaxed, his mouth slightly open. He seemed younger. Ray looked at him for a long time, seeing the pores, the lines beside his mouth, the sagging skin beneath his eyes. It was the first time he had ever looked at his father without being afraid.

Ray loved him.

Tough People

The bell rang for the first round and I stepped across the canvas holding the red gloves high to guard my face. The crowd was rooting for my opponent, a big Indian with plenty of reach. All I could do was duck, go inside, and go to work. I'd never fought before and I was scared.

We circled each other and I blocked two jabs, then dodged a roundhouse right. The only rules were no kicking, biting, or elbows. Blurred tattoos covered his chest and arms. He came at me again. I ducked and popped him in the face, and the jolt went up my arm and into my body. I stung him twice more the same way. My mouth was dry. It seemed like we'd been fighting for hours. He led with his jab and I ducked again, but this time he was waiting for me. His haymaker got me on the temple and I felt two days pass.

When I woke up, the cornerman was removing the gloves. He led me out of the ring to a folding chair. I sat there breathing hard, mad at myself. A little piece of my mind wondered if Lynn had run off with the guy who'd beat me, but I knew that was bad luck talking in my head. Bad luck was how I got here, and now my luck had dipped again.

Lynn dropped into the chair beside me. She doesn't sit in a regular way. She gets near a chair and lets gravity pull her onto the seat. It's her only bad habit.

"Are you hurt?" she said.

"I'll have a shiner."

"I wish I took some pictures."

"Where you been?"

"I signed up for tomorrow."

"I'm out of it. You only get one chance."

"Not you," she said. "I signed up for the Tough Woman Contest."

"No way."

"Way," she said. "There's only three women so I'm automatically in the finals. I get five hundred bucks for stepping in the ring. We can go back to Billings."

She and I had been traveling together before we went broke here in Great Falls. Entering the Montana Tough Man Contest had seemed like a good way to raise bus fare out of town. Now it just seemed stupid.

Lynn held my arm as we walked to the motel, and after a quick shower, we put that mattress through its paces. I guess the main reason we were together was sex. I know that has a bad sound to it, like we're just wild, but that's not exactly true. I'd left Kentucky a while back and was a cook at the same diner where she worked as a waitress. She was a photographer, but had pawned her camera to cover our motel bill. We'd been hanging out for two weeks. We got along okay. We talked. It's just that our bodies could sing.

In the morning my eye was puffed and black as a burnt biscuit. I'm not even an athlete, let alone a fighter, and my body was pretty sore. Lynn went out for coffee while I took a long bath. The notion of her fighting for money went against my raisings. It made me feel responsible for her and I didn't want that. Neither of us did. We just wanted to be free.

She came back to the room and held her hands in front of her face, thumbs touching, fingers pointing up. She tilted her head and squinted. It was how she practiced taking pictures.

"That would make a good photograph," she said. "The boxer in the tub."

"I don't want you to fight," I said.

"It's not up to you."

"I ain't trying to tell you what to do, Lynn. Going broke was my fault and I hate you had to hock your camera."

"Get off it," she said. "I bought it used. I'll get a better one next."

"We could sell our blood," I said. "Maybe volunteer for medical tests."

"It'll take too long. I can make a half a grand in three minutes."

"It just ain't right. A woman ain't supposed to fight for a man."

"What's fair for you is fair for me. Besides, I might win. We'll get two thousand cash and have a great life. This is just a rough patch. Even rich people have it rough sometimes."

"I reckon."

"Let's pretend we are rich," she said. "Let's just think that way and act accordingly."

"First thing is to get a fancy camera."

"I'll take a thousand pictures of you a day. That's like twenty-five rolls."

I got out of the tub and dried myself while she practiced taking pictures, squatting to change angles, and making a whirring sound as she advanced the film. Even though she was faking, I felt embarrassed by a nude shot.

"Let's go to Seattle," she said. "Everybody I know is moving there."

"It's your money."

"No, it's ours. There's better jobs there."

We laughed and talked and made plans to open a photo gallery and diner in Seattle. It would be old style, with good food cheap. Lynn's pictures would hang on the walls, and the menu would be shaped like a negative with holes along the side. We'd have specials called F-Stop Burger, and Zoom Lens Soup. Photographers and Kentuckians could eat there free.

Lynn needed rest and I took a walk. The sky was haired over solid grey. There was no sun, just a dull light, and I figured snow was coming. Great Falls reminded me of towns in Kentucky that hadn't changed since the fifties. The buildings were low and made of stone, and people strolled from store to store. I thought about home and wished I'd never left. Kentucky's idea of a tough man contest is to get through the season at hand.

In a pawnshop window was a camera that came with a bunch of lenses. I wanted to buy it all and go back to the room and throw the whole rig on the bed. That would make Lynn and me square. I hated the idea of owing somebody. I stood there for a long time thinking that having money gave you freedom, but getting the money took freedom away. What I needed was luck.

I started worrying that Lynn might get hurt in the fight, break her nose or lose a tooth—and blame me. The more I thought about it, the madder I got.

Inside I felt like I was about to bust, but there was nowhere for me to go with it.

I went back to the motel and stopped at the bar. It was called the Sip & Dip, and had a tropical decor with plastic parrots, bamboo walls, and fake torches. Any minute you expected a cannibal to jump out at you. An older couple was arguing at a table shaped like a kidney bean. A tall man about forty came in, ordered a whiskey ditch, and began talking to me. He was from Mississippi. His southern accent made me feel good, as if I were talking to a countryman.

"Luck always turns," he said. "There's nothing you can do when you're running bad but develop yourself a leather ass. How did you happen to be here for the Tough Man Contest?"

"I borrowed a car from a guy at work. Me and Lynn wanted to get out of Billings and run around."

He told the bartender to bring a couple of drinks.

"On me," he said. "You're a guy who needs a lot of outs right now."

"You know I can't buy the next round."

"There was a time when all I owned was on my back. So you and Lynn were on the loose."

"Yeah," I said. "We had a couple hundred bucks and four days off from work. We're thinking maybe we'll hit the Chico Hot Springs when bang, we're pulled over by the Highway Patrol. I'm sober and we're not carrying dope, so I'm not worried. I'm good with cops, I say yes sir and no sir, and all that. They have a tough job. I respect that because my job ain't the best. When you're a cook, everything will cut you or burn you."

He said he understood. The older couple who'd been arguing were kissing now, pecking at each other's faces like a pair of chickens.

"Do you live here?" I said.

"No. I have a cabin up in Big Sandy. I'll do some bird hunting this week."

"There's a river in Kentucky with the same name."

"I suppose that's possible," he said. He looked at me like he was gauging worth. "Is Lynn beautiful?"

"Definitely."

"Beautiful women make me fear death."

I sat and studied on that for a while. Dying never scared me, but life does every day. I couldn't tell him that, though. I wondered if he was sick with some disease, or maybe he was older than I thought.

"What's your name," I said.

"Jack," he said. "Jack King. I'm in the deck."

"I don't get you."

"A deck of cards."

"Is that your real name?"

He gave the bartender the sign for more drinks. The older couple had quit smooching and seemed to be resting. Keno machines blinked in the corner.

"I'm a gambler," Jack said. "I've been down to those riverboats in Louisiana for quite some time. I like to come up here and hunt and play a little poker."

"Whereabouts do you play?"

"The Butte game goes all night."

"Is that what you like?"

"The minute you sit down, you have to be willing to play for days. You could learn from that."

"What do you mean?" I said.

"You need to cowboy up."

"I'm doing the best I can. It just don't feel right to have your girlfriend out fighting for money."

"I once had a girlfriend who worked as a dancer

in a topless joint. It was the worst two weeks of my life, but she made a bankroll to choke a horse. We had a nice run."

He twisted a heavy gold ring, and I noticed that he wore them on the last two fingers of each hand. He spoke without looking at me. "You never finished telling about that cop pulling you over."

"Well, that's when everything just went to hell in a handcart. The guy I borrowed the car from had stolen it. The cops held me in jail for three days until they found him. Lynn had to stay in a motel. When I got out, we pretty much blew the rest of our money at karaoke night downtown."

Behind the bar was a glass window that looked into the deep end of the motel pool. You couldn't see past the surface of the water, which made the swimmers seem headless. A pair of pale legs floated past the window and I recognized them as belonging to Lynn. She wore a black one-piece. I liked watching her, knowing she didn't know I was there.

The older couple was working on another drink. He was singing to her, one of those old songs you don't hear anymore, and I imagined Lynn and me still together at their age. Jack was right. Things were about to change.

"In your line," I said, "you must learn a lot about luck."

"I knew a gambler who ran into a losing streak for three months down in Reno. By the end of it, he'd sold his watch, ring, and belt buckle. He owed money to everyone he knew. He sublet his place and slept in his car. Then he sold his car and kept playing. Out of the blue he got so lucky he could piss in a swinging jug. Won a hundred grand in two days."

"Wow," I said.

I wondered if Jack's story was about himself. He told it in a personal way, as if recounting the good old days.

"Tell me," he said, "do people bet on these fights?"

"I don't know."

"Seeing as how you're on the ankle express, I'll give you a ride over there. Meet me in the lobby at six-thirty."

He left and I wished I could go somewhere and start all over, which is how I've felt all my life. As soon as I get somewhere, I'm ready to leave. I finished my drink and went back to the room, where Lynn was sitting in bed. There was an intent look on her face that I'd only seen during the height of breakfast rush at the diner.

"Hey," I said, "I got us a ride."

"Borrow another car?"

"I met this guy who said he'd give us a lift. You'll like him."

"I'm not in a frame of mind to like anyone."

"You don't have to fight."

"I don't see any choice."

"We can get restaurant jobs here. In a month we'll be in Seattle."

"I don't care about Seattle," she said. "I just want out of this hotel, this town, and everything else. I don't care how."

She looked at me like I was her enemy. I could see she wanted privacy so I stayed in the bathroom until time to meet Jack. I didn't know if she was getting mad because she had to fight, or so she could fight. Either way, it gave me a bad feeling.

We met Jack in the lobby at six, and when I introduced them, she wouldn't talk. We went outside to his car. I'd never been in a Cadillac before and it was not something I minded. I've heard they can go anywhere a pickup can go. We followed the Missouri River to a filling station with a store attached. I asked if he wanted me to gas it up, and he shook his head and went inside. Lynn stared through the windshield at a neon sign that glowed orange. I tried to think of something to say. Jack came back with two quarts of water, an energy bar, a box of band-aids, and a ballpoint pen. He made Lynn eat and drink.

We parked at the fairgrounds and walked across the lot to the arena. Jack was talking to her in a low voice, his arm across her shoulders like a coach. It was a nice night, the clear sky covered by stars like dew. At times I missed Kentucky, but never at night. When I couldn't see the land out there, I forgot I wasn't at home. Sometimes I wished it was always night.

We checked Lynn in, then went to the fighters' area, which was just some metal chairs in the corner. The center of the arena held a boxing ring on a platform, surrounded by rows of people who'd paid extra to sit close. Along two sides were rising sets of bleachers. The lights gleamed above the ring. Jack used three band-aids to build a strip across Lynn's nose, holding it open to get more air. He told her not to drink the water yet, and walked away. I sat beside her.

"You scared?" I said.

"Yes," she said. "Jack said it was okay to be scared. He said if I wasn't, there was something wrong with me."

"There's nothing wrong with you."

"I don't want to get hurt."

"The gloves are thick and the headgear covers you. Plus women wear that belly pad."

"They're still hitting you."

"The time goes fast, Lynn."

I looked away when I said that because it was a big fat lie. That round I fought was the slowest minute of my life. It felt like a month of Sundays.

"Whatever happens," I said, "you just remember I'm right here and I always will be."

She looked at me with an odd expression on her face, then stood and began to stretch. I walked to the concession stand. The arena was jammed with Indians and I looked them over carefully. They dressed like people in the hills at home—flannel shirts, jeans, boots, and work jackets—men and women alike. Quite a few wore glasses. I thought maybe Indians just had bad eyes, until I remembered that a lot of people at home wore glasses because they couldn't afford contact lenses. I wondered if it was the same here.

The first bout had just ended. The fighters left the ring to sit with their families. Smoking was not allowed, but you could drink beer, and a few people were already staggering. A couple of young men gave me dirty looks for being white, until they saw my black eye. Then they said hello.

The guy who knocked me out stopped and shook my hand. He was a little bit drunk. His name was Alex. He wore a rodeo buckle and fancy cowboy boots. His long braids were tied together behind his neck.

"I lost the last fight last night," he said.

"I didn't see it."

"Came all the way from Browning to find a man who hits as hard as my horse kicks."

"Well," I said, "ours was a good fight."

"You got your licks in."

"You won it."

"Yes," he said, "even a blind squirrel finds a nut sometimes."

The P.A. announced the women's finals. When I got to Lynn, Jack was already there, rubbing her shoulders and whispering in her ear. He'd used the pen he'd bought to write on her fists. Her left hand carried the word "kiss," and her right hand said "kill." He was telling her to jab with the left, kissing her opponent on the mouth, then kill her with the right.

We walked Lynn to the ring. She wasn't blinking.

"Go for the face," Jack said. "Keep your chin down and your eyes open. Circle but don't back up. Say this over and over—kiss, kiss, kill."

She nodded and climbed the stepladder to the ring. The other fighter was a short Indian woman with a powerful body. I knew Lynn would lose and I felt awful for having put her there. If I hadn't left Kentucky, she'd be with a guy who had more to offer.

The bell rang. The crowd was yelling, and the announcer chanted into his microphone, "Here kitty, kitty, kitty." The Indian woman moved slowly, waiting to see what Lynn would do. Lynn's little white legs looked pathetic below the torso pad. She wore her swimsuit, and I wished she was still in the pool, that they were fighting in the water where Lynn would have a chance. They circled each other three times. Jack stood beside me muttering, "Kiss, kiss, kill."

The people in the crowd were yelling for blood. Lynn's fists were up and her chin was down, and suddenly she jumped through the air, swinging both fists wildly at the woman's head. Lynn connected two or three times before the woman shoved her away and hit her in the face, opening a cut above her eye. When I saw the red smear, my guts just folded up on themselves.

The doctor called time and the referee took the fighters to neutral corners. The doctor examined the cut, put ointment on it, and left the ring. Lynn had a look I'd seen when a customer stiffed her at the diner. She was mad. The other woman just looked serious, like she could face a sideways ice storm and walk all night. She moved forward a step at a time. Everybody in the place understood that Lynn was no fighter, but she was in there, and she wasn't afraid.

The Indian woman walked to Lynn as if to shake hands and hit her very hard on the cut eye. Lynn's head jerked to the side, spattering blood on the canvas floor of the ring. I started to cry. When I looked up, the fight was over. The doctor had stopped it and the crowd was booing.

The doctor worked on the cut while a man from the judge's table handed Lynn an envelope. Jack helped her to a chair. He held her chin with one hand and lifted the water to her mouth like a baby's bottle. He was very gentle. I sat beside Lynn. She was gasping for breath, her chest rising and falling, barely able to drink. There was a butterfly bandage across her left eyebrow. A sheen of sweat covered her skin.

"The doctor said it won't scar," Jack said.

"I want it to," she said.

The woman who won the fight leaned over the chair to hug Lynn. Her arms were strong, with raised scars on them. The two women reeked of sweat in a way that I had only smelled on men in a work crew. They whispered in each other's ears. After Lynn got control of her breathing, Jack helped her to the rest room where she could change clothes.

I sat there thinking that Lynn was tougher than me. She hadn't gone down, she'd just got cut. I watched the winner walk the aisle. Someone gave

her a cup of beer and someone else gave her a cigarette and I suddenly wanted her for a girlfriend. I
wanted to treat her as tenderly as Jack had treated
Lynn. The woman was beautiful in the garish lights
of the ring that spilled shadows on the bleachers.
Whatever she'd gone through to get so tough
soaked me with sorrow.

Lynn and Jack joined me. The flush had faded
from her skin. She'd wet her face and hair, and she
looked fine. We went outside, past teenage boys
smoking cigarettes and faking punches at each
other. The dry cold air snapped against my face.
Snow drifted down, one of those early autumn
snows before the hard cold sets in. The flakes were
the size of silver dollars falling from the sky, turning the black night white.

"If they hadn't stopped it," I said, "you'd have
won. It was your fight."

"No, it wasn't," Lynn said. "It was never my
fight."

Jack unlocked the Cadillac and sat behind the
wheel. Lynn gave me the envelope that contained
her prize money.

"I'm going with Jack," she said. "I'm sorry."

I nodded.

"The motel is paid through tomorrow," she said. "We can drop you there, if you want."

I shook my head no.

"This isn't about you," she said. "This is about me."

She hugged me then, squeezing me tighter than she ever had. My face pushed against her neck and I smelled the cheap soap from the rest room. I put my arms around her, but I couldn't hug back. My knees felt wobbly. She stepped away. She was sad but trying to smile. A strand of hair fell over her face. I lifted my hands and pretended to take a picture.

She got in the car and I watched the red taillights move around a corner.

I headed for the motel and stopped at the bridge that crossed the Missouri River. I stood there a long time. Snow was thick in the air. My family had been in the hills for two hundred years and I was the first to leave. Now I was pretty much ruined for going back. The black water ran fast and cold below.

I started walking.

A History of the Type

The typeface used in this book is Fournier, an early transitional type designed by Pierre Simon Fournier *le jeune* (1712–1768), the great Parisian punchcutter, founder, printer, and inventor of the point system upon which modern measurement is based. The digital version seen here is a rendering of the Monotype Corporation's 1925 design of Fournier's *St. Augustin ordinaire* type, with shortened capitals relative to the height of the ascenders. Markedly influenced by the *Roman du roi* typeface of 1702, Fournier displays the contrast in weight of hair-stroke and stem and the flattened serif characteristic of other transitional types such as Baskerville, Bell, and Caledonia.